To two very special names

Patrick

'Barbai

Graham Burgess

PRDS: PARADISE, THE SECRET GARDEN

Limited Special Edition. No. 24 of 25 Paperbacks

One time ran through half of the Kew Gardens; one time Director with John Lewis Partnership; designer of a wide range of landscapes including symbolic mazes. Expert in ancient symbolism and use of images and words to tune into the subconscious.

Dedicated to the ghosts who are, in fact, my 'well done hosts'.

Graham Burgess

PRDS: Paradise, the Secret Garden

AUSTIN MACAULEY PUBLISHERS™

LONDON • CAMBRIDGE • NEW YORK • SHARJAH

A CIP catalogue record for this title is available from the British Library.

ISBN 9781528928373 (Paperback)
ISBN 9781528965453 (ePub e-book)

www.austinmacauley.com

First Published (2019)
Austin Macauley Publishers Ltd
25 Canada Square
Canary Wharf
London
E14 5LQ

Meeting Ghosts

This book is not simple. It contains secrets that have been in place for hundreds of years being exposed. That is not to say they have been hidden, but quite the opposite. They have been secrets on full view and such a thing is called a rebus.

An ancient Hebrew concept called PRDS alludes to it and that is based on a story called Paradise, The Secret Garden. No vowels in Hebrew, so take them out and we have another step along the code-route PRDS.

> *P* stands for PRADASH (surface meaning)
> *R* stands for REMEZ (hint at something below the surface)
> *D* stands for DRASHA (allegorical story not to be taken literally)
> *S* stands for SOD (hidden)

The book reveals SOD on many levels and that is the first part of the book.

The rest of the book is The Appendix and this empowers one to better understand how the secrets have been complied so you can go on to discover more or even invent your own rebuses.

The Appendix provides proofs.

A key aspect is The Book of Letters, revealing how the English Alphabet in uppercase tunes into basic concepts of meaning.

The English Alphabet is very simple in its construction and this efficiency is leading to its adoption worldwide. All the letters are made up from straight lines at angles and half-curves (arch angles).

The letter *G* is made up from a letter *C*, which means 'capable of creation' but its curving round is topped before it becomes the *O* of birthing and a letter *T* which means 'of substance in this reality' is attached. The letter *G* means 'well done'.

So, what if we look at a certain word and ask what it means?

We are very clear everyday what a HOST is, but what is a GHOST?

The book is about my meeting with a group of people, all of whom are dead. Their intellectual energies and creative skills have not passed away; they are all around us and to a great extent affecting our lives.

So rich is what they have created that the last thing we experience when we tune into their work is their death. They continue to be well-done hosts.

My book is based on a visualised invitation from them and of course one must feel honoured.

I think the reason I have been involved is that they think that what they have expressed is of key on-going value and there is a need to ensure it is conserved for the right reasons and applied to future investments.

The first part of the book is simple text and key pictures of the GHOSTS and what they have done.

This book is a collection of concepts that will hopefully entertain you and also allow you to enter into different realities.

A basic concept is PARADISE, THE SECRET GARDEN. Another key focus is on what is called a REBUS. A rebus is a secret that is not actually hidden; it is on full view.

In ancient Hebrew, there were no vowels, so PARADISE becomes PRDS.

Then a code is applied.

P stands for Pradash which means 'surface meaning'.

R stands for REMEX which means 'hint of something below the surface'.

D stands for DRASHA. It may be allegorical story not to be taken literally.

S stands for SOD which is the secret.

So this book is about applying this in many areas.

It will expose a number of secrets in works of art that are universally known and enjoyed on various levels.

Another key factor is deeper exploration of the way we use lines to create our alphabet and other creative configurations.

My Amazing Visit

I opened an amazing door. Over the door, a zigzag of letter *W*, so often seen on entry to sacred places. Inside, a special room and a gathering of special hosts.

I said, "You have all revealed realities that are core to the quality of life so many human beings enjoy, due to what they have inherited from you. My personal enrichment came from various mentors and my experience of epilepsy between the age of nine and sixteen years when as a small boy I discovered transcendental meditation but more than anything from what Randoll Coate linked me to many years later. Your evolution, Randoll, of the modern symbolic labyrinth or maze took a step deeper into the matrix of understanding and being creative in respect of expressing realities."

Claude Monet and Marc Chagall came over and embraced me with tears in their eyes and they said they knew of the passing of my Gillian. Tears arise whenever the human brain is overcome with emotions positive or negative and then one's eyes are washed with the purest fluid on earth as a signal we want to see things more clearly. The next benefit is that those who care may see them and ask, "Why are you crying?" and shared healing may result. I know why they responded in respect of Lost Love as deeply as they did, as you will come to understand later.

Dear mentors, I have put a lot of thought into the structuring of this book as it is complicated but I want to tune in with my relationship, as shared with you and the new readers, in the best way so some preparation, almost like an apprenticeship, needs to be employed.

The book is not normal in that the most effective value will be from reading a few pages in normal sequence and then referring to the Appendix where one can gain some deeper understanding in particular areas. It may result in links that none of us are aware of being exposed. I am reminded of a deeply symbolic garden I did at the first Hampton Court Palace Flower Show and a man called Derek Jarman came along and said, "You have written a story and we have come here to tell it to you."

What you, dear mentors, have contributed over very many years is presented according to topic, not a rigid timeline, so the layout of the book echoes this.

I do not think you were able to forecast this meeting Nostrodamus as the content has been so effectively hidden from most people.

A rebus is a secret that is not hidden; it is on full view. You may share some and go on to realise more.

I have a horticultural background and this has long been a part of man's symbolic expression. The mosaic in Hisham's Palace three kilometres north of Jericho and compiled around 724-743 BC has a hint, namely one of the deer in the picture is not in touch with the points of green that represent life-giving forces. It is about to die. The symbolic message there is: "Keep in touch with the forces of Nature." In Sanskrit, May means little points, the little points of new growth. So later, "Ne'er cast your clout till May is out," i.e. when the little shoots are open leaves.

Readers will see how this has been applied in the works of my kindred spirits.

Another chapter in the Appendix will help them understand how I approach our very efficient alphabet.

Like so many other creations, the book exists as a tool and most people who use the tool know little of its make-up. One need not know the details behind a tool's make-up so long as it performs useful functions.

Networks are important. If you want to catch fish, you create a rectilinear network and so long as the gap between the components is smaller than the fish you may catch it.

The English Alphabet is a relatively simple arrangement of lines. My analysis is based on alphabet in uppercase, as lower was only introduced to speed up the writing process. All the letters are made up from straight lines placed at ANGLES and half curves or ARCH ANGLES. Those of you who are French will know us as Les Anglais. The letter designs are very simple and the statistically most used letter is the letter *E*. It looks like a shelving system and the intuit of its inner meaning is 'capable of taking in, holding and giving out energy and information'. Wherever one wishes to emphasise the intuit, one multiplies the number of letters used in a word. So to eat more, FEED to hear more, HEED; the go faster SPEED; require more NEED; very simple use of angles.

Read that appendix now before we move on. What will you SEE? What is a PAGE?

Randoll, you furnished me with the mind-set that led me to ask, "Why is the letter *A* at the beginning of the alphabet?" It is a question I had never thought of asking until I was sixty-six years of age.

Direction and relative-location is another device we use and whilst we employ some very simple applications of direction in formulating our alphabet or the lines of longitude and latitude. You Randoll were a master of extreme complexity, hence you invented what we call The Modern Symbolic Labyrinth, no limit to direction and it leads to multiple levels of perception. No one prior to you Randoll conceived that in such a sophisticated and inclusive way. See Appendix for History of Mazes and Labyrinths.

All this is written on a PAGE. It has been proved we see all words as pictures not totally controlled by the direction we read in. Read backwards, it explains what is happening; the EGAP allows us to access whatever is on the PAGE.

A book is rather like a letter *E* but with the upper left-hand straight line being the spine of the book. We often thumb through a book from the back and stop at a PAGE or EGAP.

"Claude, you are so close to me in so many ways. I know your horticultural interest started with you growing potatoes with Renoir in Paris when you were quite poor but eventually you indulged in gardening seriously at Giverny. I think you loved Dahlias due to the wide range of colours."

"Yes, Graham, and I know you discovered why I chose to use the Nymphaeas in my artistic explorations. What led you to it?"

"Well, Claude, it was purely practical."

I learned a lot about botany at Kew Gardens but it was not until I was a Director with a well-known English firm called The John Lewis Partnership that I was responsible for many gardens one the world's finest water garden at Longstock in Hampshire, England. You must still be so proud of the Garden Spedan.

You said, "Everyone who works in a company should share the benefits of wealth and power." It had a good collection of Nymphaeas, and later I was deeply into the horticultural trade harvesting thousands of water lilies in the winter for export to Europe.

Then I saw the photographs of your garden at Giverny Claude and the first thing that hit me were all the water lily leaves flat on the surface. Applying another form of logic, to do with levels, I noticed that the plane that one group of leaves was in, in your paintings, was not exactly the same as another. The only thing not reflected in any group of water lilies was the leaves. I know achieving this in the garden meant a lot of careful labour had been employed at some cost throughout the summer, thinning the water lilies. If they are not thinned, the leaves rise in clumps so the tops of the clumps, like small hills, are reflected. So each leaf was the only thing that we could experience definitely as part of this reality, the rest reflection and reflection, of what? Each leaf is geometrically circular, so it is in itself a paradox.

I suspect I still know little of what you reflected upon and hid in the spaces between. On a practical level, I visited your garden at Giverny and saw no lilies. Water rats had eaten them so I said when I came next I would bring replacement for water lilies.

I was welcomed by Gerald Van der Kemp and his wife, Florence, and they treated me to lunch in your blue and yellow room.

"I see you are smiling, Charles Lutwidge, and I suspect you are pleased I tuned into a similar concept you revealed through Alice Liddell and the Looking Glass. I know you met her just round the corner from Longstock in Fullerton."

She looked at a mirror with you and asked, "Can the cat drink the milk in the saucer?"

You said, "No." The question and your answer are REMEZ.

For most the story went on but an important question was: Why should this intelligent young fourteen-year-old girl ask if the cat they all knew and loved could drink milk out of the saucer? It did it every day. Her question was very intellectual and to do with whether the cat they all knew and loved could drink the milk in the saucer reflected in the mirror.

"Your scientific theory of the asymmetrical universe said that anything inorganic reflected is the same, but the organic milk was not." So the cat they all knew and loved could not drink the milk in the refection.

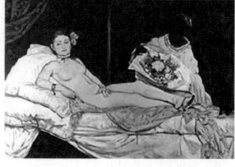

It is fascinating, Claude, how your commitment to Manet and particularly his painting of Olympia, with almost hidden cat, was underway when Bory La Tour Marliac attended The Grand Exposition in 1897.

"Claude did buy some of my Nymphaeas, although I know Claude was dissuaded from attending the exhibition because of his tussle with the establishment with regard to Olympia," said Bory.

"Your story is in the Appendix Bory and I only discovered your secret codings in the names of your Nymphaeas due to the fact that I compared the proper Latin names at Kew with the names you chose, which on the surface, sorry Claude, another surface, looked normally scientific but in fact they have other meanings, on reflection.

Because no botanist was inclined to look at the plants you raised and the horticultural trade is happy with any name that helps sell the plants; the secret remained on full view for years. Nobody questioned it. You were initially a classicist and that was another clue to what you chose as a clue in many of the names."

I spoke earlier of the skills we have in communicating with lines and of course in some art forms the complexity can hide things. In some cases, the PRDS is well used and a key is to look for the REMEZ hints.

Let us share what you Claude, you Sandro and you Marc and you Francois have hidden.

I like the way so many people have got your story in The Three Graces wrong, Sandro, right from square one. Had people realised what is concealed in your painting, it would have gone on the Bonfire of the Vanities together with other works associated with sex and gambling. Tell me if I am wrong.

On the right, Aeolus has organised a wind-god to come in from the east. That's the direction we always get the sun from and it brings us light so we can see things. So reading from right to left in many paintings is how we link with the PAGE or in reverse EGAP. He is a gust and he is using that energy to bring in a young female, Chloris. Gust is OK, as is lust, so long as the energy is properly controlled. She looks back in trepidation and holds her hand out in trepidation. In her mouth was a small sprig of green, the green being one of the oldest hints at the life force. In ancient Sanskrit, Maes meant 'little points', the little points of new growth. "So ne'er cast your clout till May is out." When the leaves are fully out. The mosaic story again.

She wears a dress symbolic of virginity and if we look at the bottom of her white dress, it is hymenal. Her journey is the opposite of the deer in the mosaic about to be separated from the green. She is soon to be awash with green and life.

Time passes and we see the same lady later standing with a good deal of confidence. She is flowering profusely and ready for the next stage. She exposes her thigh which is symbolic of her vagina and as you can see, she has not yet been de-flowered. Another clue is the bottom of her dress that is still hymenal. In the background, another lady watches what is going on. She is the mother and she has seen it happen before. She also holds her hand out to the west with some care. She has been through it all and sees that the bottom of her dress is flopped and it is red. She has given birth before. She knows what is happening because she senses another individual, seldom seen. It is Cupid and he is as ever flying about. He is about to let loose an arrow. He is blindfolded as he cares not who gets to fall in love.

One less eye than you're playing Cupid Claude. Look up the meaning of EYE. Another key essence of Nature he is subscribing to is variation and bio-diversity.

The Three Graces are one person in different stages.

The arrow is about to be released as in the dance-of-life she has left one position turned and returned. The latter is rematio, to return, as in Greek and an important ancient belief that one only learns certain things when one returns. The arrow is pointed directly to her heart. She is about to fall in love with the seductive guy to the west.

Manet added, "I used your flower, Sandro, as a model for the one I put in Olympia as the lady comes to flower Olympia. What you have to decide is whether the lady on the couch is a prostitute or the young lady at a stage between Chloris and Flora and the lady behind is the mother preparing her child."

Is she bringing the flowers or taking them away for application elsewhere later?

I will return to you Claude and what the striking of the arrow can imbue. Your love for Camille Doncieux was so strong. Often she is twice in your paintings and I know you shared with Cezanne the story of you hidden in the dappled shade as another cherub with one large eye. Hinting at the power many previous people had if they had one eye. Odin etc.

"I said he is one big eye but are you the only other one who knew what I was talking about Graham?" said Cezanne.

"It is something we were all aware of," said Rembrandt. "I posed with one eye in one of my drawings and as you know I shed many tears following the early deaths of my three baby girls."

The arrow struck you twice, Claude, as you fell for Alice Hoschede and I know you struggled financially, with Camille and Alice sharing dresses on different days when they went into Paris. Then this awful thing, death, Camille died young.

She still lives with you however and my understanding of the reflective approach you made in your impressionism led me to see her body as you hid it in the waters. John Everett Millais did it in a more obvious way. Carnea is the pink of flesh and an early name you gave to one of your Nymphaeas Bory.

The looking at things from different angle is simply expressed in your picture of her on her deathbed. It was one day in Paris with you Randoll, looking at the painting as you will remember, when I learned that one has to turn the picture upside down to see her being re-born.

The same structure but a different message when you change the angle of viewing:

 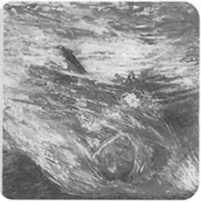

What makes me cry more than that, Claude, is to do with the story of the tryst trees you planted.

I explain more of TRYST PLANTING in the appendix but when they blew over what you said to Madame Le Fells makes me weep more than any willow. When the gardeners cut the tops off they resurrected as willows often do.

It is interesting how the energies of lust, love and passion have been celebrated through art in so many ways. An old name for Willow is saille and sails on ships harness the gusts of wind. I know you, Alexander, planted some special weeping willows by the river at your house in Twickenham, derived from a basket full of figs brought from Turkey and that led to all the weeping willows in America. The same term saille is applied to the uprights in wattle hurdles, again symbolic of harnessing forces to bring benefits.

In Gerard's Herbal, there are only two plants that suppress lust. One is the melon and the other is the water lily.

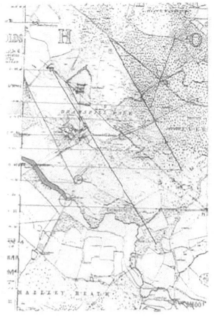

An early name for garden was gyrdan, a girdle or fence and the shepherd's favourite hurdle was made from wood with ten vertical sailles. Maybe willow but sometimes the hazel which represented wisdom and the origin of 'tell me in a nutshell'. So another saille designed to control external forces to bring on-going benefits, this time not the wind but livestock, either keeping them in or out.

If you have absorbed the intuits in the Alphabet Appendix, you will see how the word ART is based on 'in our perceived existence *A*' with 'intense external energies *R*' and an end result of 'substance in this reality *T*'.

It's all lines. The British Rock has tuned into some line-making from the past and exposing other lines. http://www.circleoffriendship.co.uk/

Your creation of Bramshill Lord Zouche has always amazed me. How come the so-called Latitude document, done by Samuel Dunn in 1717, is actually more than the one latitude in the title, a remez, and the numbers referred to link to the points on the 1850 map, key to the underlying geometry installed in 1604.

The positioning of the house is a special number from the old maze site and the house is very much in the Vetruvian style which your dear friend Henry Wotton translated in Rome for us.

You did say Henry,

"A diplomat is a politician that goes abroad to tell lies on behalf of his country."

You may have done that but your translation of the works of Vetruvius had a massive effect on our landscape as people tried to recreate the Roman symbolic landscapes.

I love your poetry also.

Have you left your body on the island in the Fish Pond Lord Zouche?

"You need to have a look Graham."

"And what did you get up to on the Hanky Panky Island? Your River Tiber is overgrown with muddy vegetation but the island is still visible on one of the old maps."

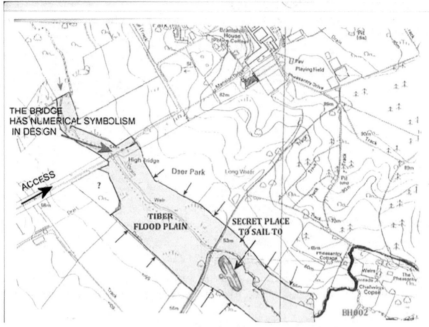

Was it an echo of the island you painted, Francois?

You have the Roman Bridge, as at Bramshill, but the buildings in the background and the mountains look like Italy.

It is another story moving from right to left. A couple of innocent infants are close to the watery and fluid stream of lust and their cuddling is so innocent. The young girl being seduced has a part flowery dress but it is not until later when she is cavorting with the gentleman that she is more flowery and open to de-flowering. I know you, Cezzane, painted Leda being seduced by a Swan, Zeus, so who is enjoying the swan songs in the edge of the water? I wonder whether the dog below has just noticed a cat coming, or is it you or me. It would be nice if the Hanky Panky Island at Bramshill was restored.

I did design a River Tiber Lake for a couple, moved by the fact that for their ruby wedding anniversary she did not want a ruby; she wanted a lake.

Years later, they invited me over to see two swans who had moved in, very appropriate to them. Birds I know were associated with all sorts of oracular messages, mostly based on clues as to what season is ambient. We still say, "A little birdie told me."

So many GODS and GODDESSES. DOG is GOD reversed so only another way of experiencing something of value.

"A question, Eduard, you are wearing a mouche as so often one sees in the records and I am wondering whether you left the one you are wearing in your wardrobe so that it influenced Cecil 12th Baron Zouche when he built Parham House?"

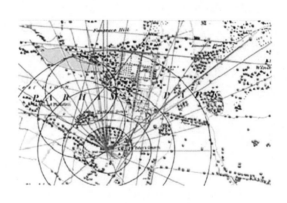

A Zouche mouche emanating from a well and forming a lovely forest
Above it is Fan Grove Hill.

There is a Tryst Planting also.

The underlying geometry is there and some hint, maybe at Alexander Pope, in Pope's Avenue but could that have been an input from Cecil 5th Baronet or Cecil 6th Baronet of Parham as they were alive when you, Alexander, were around expounding your intellectual cleverness?

I always look for wells and wellness.

When I did the Labyrinth of Love for Lord Bath, I did not do a sacred geometry analysis but when he asked me to do The Maze of Chance, I said we really ought to re-explore, rematio. I discovered the house and gardens geometry all starts from a well that was in the Cistercian Monastery before the house was built. Wherever I see well or fishpond on old maps, I wonder whether it is a REMEZ.

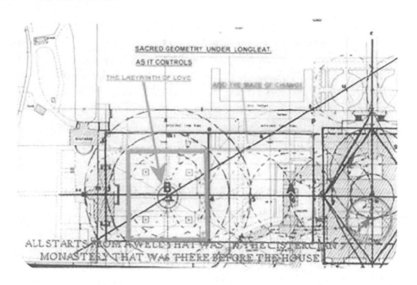

All rematio but sometimes one discovers by accident.

I grew up an active Christian and my aunty Kath gave me a book to reinforce my beliefs. It was The Bible as History and it sought to prove that what is written in the Bible is based on fact. The miracle of the burning-bush then moved to what happens naturally amongst zerophytic plants in desert areas where the heat would boil water and kill the plant, where sap comprised of volatile oils was safer. That book sat in my library for years and my understanding of what it said changed little until one day I was in the great house at Stowe and I noticed an old plan on the wall. The shape of the enclosing layout reminded me of an image in the book so when I got home, rematio, I searched for the image. There in the text it refers to a circle of points placed around Jerusalem at the time of the invasion by Titus in 70 AD. I counted to see if the number of points mentioned in the text matched those on the plan. They did not, so another REMEZ. I then applied geometry to the points and discovered that Stowe is based on the geometry of Jerusalem at the time of the invasion by Titus. It is also based on nine great circles.

So what you wrote, Alexander, "Consult the Genius of the Place" hints at what one ought to do to go through PRDS. In your text, you hint at so many things including the geometry.

If you read the title on the map and every word, you get one message.

A Plan of the House & Gardens of the Right Honourable Earl Temple Visc & Baron Cobham at Stowe in Buckinghamshire. If you read what is within it, in italics, you see what it is, namely Plan of the Royal Temple at Stowe in Buckinghamshire. This twisting of the letter format was revealed in one of the old garden guides.

A wonderful example of REMEZ, hint of something below the surface

Once whilst stopping with Schlomo Shmeruk in Jerusalem, he who chaired the committee that built the Hebrew University, I met up co-incidentally with the world expert on old maps of Jerusalem and he did not know of the inspiring map.

ITALIC, ITALY Vetruvian Architecture. Yes, Capability installed a Modern English Landscape Style Landscape at Stowe but he was not allowed to let it interfere with the earlier geometries. There is River Tiber and an island but the Hanky Panky also went on for those who did not want to explore cerebral interests this time in the Temple above, in the rock caves. The old meaning of STOW is 'sacred place'. When I was asked to do a Knot Garden for Southwark Cathedral, other things were revealed. Until 1912, it was called Our Lady of the Ovaries alluding to the Almond's fertility and its association with The Magdalen. Kew training again helping as the Latin name of the almond is Prunus amygdalus. North of Jerusalem Magdala, where Mary met Jesus, is full of almond orchards. Part of the wall that divides the cathedral

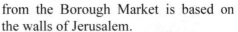

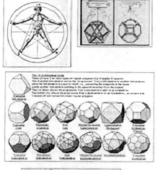

from the Borough Market is based on the walls of Jerusalem.

Water flows through my life and rock also plays a role. Is the rock under a trap door in the church next door to Bramshill the point from which the geometry started?

Bramshill has some very sophisticated components.

The Troco Stone is said to be part of game but I believe it is a key part of a symbolic, generative, sexual, organ of the Vetruvian Man on whom the house is modelled, more based on Cesarianus' earlier model.

The geometry of The Troco Stone is outstanding. It is a rhombododecahedron with each of the sides seven inches long and a sundial on one side.

It is a step on from the basic Archimedian Solids. It has been moved around and damaged which is a pity.

In a garden restoration I did some years ago at Bramshill, I discovered lots of sacred geometry and tried to consolidate it and not remove it. The plants planted would have been available to Lobel, close friend of yours, Eduard.

I think the old saying "Proportion is more important than scale" is so relevant at Bramshill. The journey of The British Rock tuned into some very basic things. First of all Rock. The boulder given by Bluestone Ltd was selected by Gillian and myself in the Preseli Mountains, home of the sacred stones in Stonehenge. The full story is in the Appendix but the hidden threads vary – Rock, Henges, Gardens, Octagons, Special numbers, Military connections, Royal links, Lines of longitude latitude, leylines, Kew Gardens and Friendship.

The longer a distance we have to travel, the more important time is. The journey of the rock has revealed to me the origin of OK and all connected with one of the threads in the rock's journey, namely Kew Gardens. Time was adjusted on clocks that had been specially placed all over the world, for example Halifax in Canada, to support our colonial economies and when the time was correct OK was put on the document. Observatory Kew.

Your involvement at Kew Decimus was full of harmony. In my first six months there as a student, I was with Mr Mac Donald. Hi, Mac. Yes, a horticulturalist but also an Egyptologist, like your father, Decimus. He gave me another book called The Rise and Decline of the Roman Religion. Interestingly, Mac corrected, by hand, errors made by the expert who wrote it.

It was not until many years later I discovered Decimus what you had done in respect of honouring Egyptology and the cleverness they applied in building.

You were a numbered child and your father gave you your first job at Regent's Park, when you were eighteen in eighteen eighteen (1818).

The age you were Aristotle when you moved to Athens. The number of ISIS, she who has a thousand names, all associated with creativity and the first oxygen breathed on Earth was O18, not what we breathe now, O2.

Basically, it is a female number as are all the even numbers. Why? One cat, one dog, one human being, one number going nowhere until: "You add another." A creative essence!

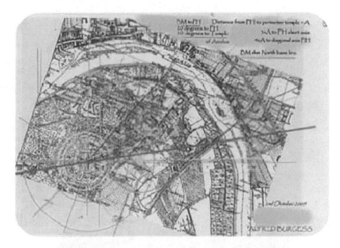

So at a time when there was an alignment of the inner planets in 1844, you did the designs for Kew. On the old map, the old Kew Bridge had a central roadway eighteen feet wide with thirty-three-inch pathways on either side. You went to the old benchmark (gone) and drew a line ten degrees south. Then you moved William Chamber's Temple of Aeolus to sit on that line. Respect for the wind again. Another ten degrees and that reached to the centre of the Palm House. A line forty-four degrees west of north provided the axis for this wonderful building.

The panels welcome us to the main gates and each panel has eighteen stars in it. In the first panel on the right, the eleventh spike is two inches lower celebrating eleven the cyclic number of the sun, the period of sunspot activity.

At the bottom between the tenth and eleventh uprights one of the spikes at the bottom was omitted, so you cleverly made your point by omitting it. REMEZ. Lots of other elevens in the gates and you re-designed the Aeroid House to have eleven windows with eighteen panes. Lots of eighteens also.

The Palm House is full of numerical symbolism celebrating the sun and the iron grids in the floor have 15 x 15 holes, fifteen being the number of The Green Man. The panes of glass celebrate '15' also. Same number of fruits on the mosaic tree and the number of males sitting on the bankh as they rowed the ancient Egyptian punt. All we see, think, eat and drink is kept in a safe box, our skull. Twenty-two pieces. Two heads are better than one, so forty-four is important.

Green Man railings? See appendix Hampton Court Palace.

I see you are here with Richard Turner Decimus and it pleases me so much that in spite of his skills in engineering, the beautiful curves of the Palm House being outside your skills-base, you were able to work with him to produce a superb end-result. Your design for The Palmhouse is now The Temperate House and full of the same numerical richness. I see you positioned it with its centre point on the line that the Temple of Aeolus is on and orientated twenty degrees west of north.

Cambridge Cottage on Kew Green is number '37', temperature of human beings worldwide and it has columns outside with eighteen vertical simulations of reeds. There is an alignment with the nearby church and Buckingham Palace.

Plus, you and your clients tuned into an alignment of the inner planets. See Appendix.

You echoed your father's interests, Decimus, and continued until you passed on. So did you, Marc. I learned of your being brought up as and Hassidic Jew and the context of your agricultural homeland and your fathers' work with herrings fills your pictures.

The Kabballa formed a basic essence of the teaching in this onetime Russian regime.

The Hassidic religion remained a core of your inspiration as did Bella who you met in 1910 of whom you said years later. "Her silence is mine. Her eyes mine. It is as if she knows everything about my childhood, my present, my future, as if she can see right through me." She died in September 1944.

Later, you married Valentina (Vava) Brodsky, not arising from a ménage-a-trois as you had Claude with Alice and Camille; and so far as I can see her attitude of persuasion led to you, on the surface, to abandoning aspects of your Hassidic upbringing.

I know you still celebrated it and realisation of that started when one day I was in Chichester Cathedral with my partner Gillian and a guide was explaining the stories in your window. She spoke of what she thought was the complete story, namely what the church had commissioned. That was PRADASH, the surface meaning but then I saw a REMEZ. It was a particular curve as in many attic sculptures, paintings and drawings. Then I saw the red it enclosed and the full picture of a Minotaur appeared.

With later analysis, the story became richer. The Minotaur is a beastly symbol but this one is not attacking, it is kneeling in obeisance. So the beast is in all of us and a key thing is to control that energy.

The right arm reaches into a purse and my botanical training told me it is the seedpod of <u>Capsella Bursa Pastoris,</u> The Shepherd's Purse. What seed is being sown? Not any cereal crop as we are standing indoors on a stone floor. It is seeds of ideas. I decided to write to the Dean, Nicholas Frayling and to support my case that one could hide such things in an image I sent him a maze design I had done after staying in one of your favourite cities, Marc, Jerusalem. My host had chaired the committee that built The Hebrew University. It was basically to make some points about my experience and the maze was based on the sacred candlestick. Jews, Gentiles and Muslims entered by different entrances but they were soon connected on the central stem. The candlestick is based on a hybrid between the Tree of Life and planetary positions. Horticulture is everywhere. At the top of the separate branches the flames and hidden in them in Hebrew text were the words light and fire. Schlomo did that for me. To

the right, the east one of the oldest and most basic gods of them all Helios shines rays and in those rays, we see the numbers sixes and sevens alluding to my interpretation of the condition then extant in Jerusalem. They were at sixes and sevens on many levels.

Turn the picture upside down and we see another beast, the wild peccary such as I experienced in the jungles of South America, thundering towards us and in front, in danger of being trodden, the two sixes upside down become two nines and eighteen, creativity.

You have to turn it upside down and that reminds me of the image Patrick Coggswell spotted in the window, based on one done by Otto Bromberger

another Parisian connection with you Marc. A figure sucking milk?

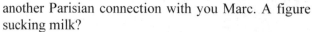

Another artist friend Sue Climpson noticed the donkey and one asks, "Is it the donkey that brought Christ into Jerusalem on its way back or is the Jewish donkey on the way out to collect their Messiah?" Only the front of the donkey is visible, so we are not sure.

Nicholas' reply stated he was at first very suspicious but now he could see things. He asked if I knew the meaning of sixes and sevens, which until he told me I did not. His father had been a member of one of the two London Guilds that could not agree who had order of precedence. In 1484, a decree was announced whereby they alternated and still do each year. He invited me to lunch and said he would wear his father's tie.

During the visit, we stood where Gillian and I had stood and he pointed to the green patch in the window and said, "I wonder about that."

It was a REMEZ and it was not until I was home a few days later that Gillian, on a connection again with John Lewis, was in a Waitrose in Andover. As she left the doors, she saw a bookshop opposite and she brought from that shop a book on the cabballa.

When I looked at some of the images, a question I had already had, the fenestration (framework) of the window, was answered. It is based on the caballa and the green patch is where Netzach, coloured green, sits. It refers to Victory.

Nicholas put my ideas to a committee and I received a letter saying Chaghall would never have included a Minotaur in a church window. Well, I know, Marc, you played the role of a Minotaur as you carried Bella in your painting 'My Beloved' and if you look closely, she is spitting at you, and in the spit another message is hidden in Hebrew script.

**CAREER
LIFE PATH
WATER**

**HEBREW
MESSAGE**

**HIDDEN IN
SPIT**

One of the reasons I am linking with you all is that you all link to common denominators and you honour them. I try to continue with it but wider communications are needed in these difficult times.

I know, Marc, that you worked on the works of Jean La Fontaine when you came to Paris and maybe the exposition of Jet d'eau could have been an inspiration. I remember discovering it in a book of his fables, when with my landscape architects hat on. I asked why the fountain in the background at the Vitruvian House, with chap being seduced by two ladies, was squirting at an angle. Maintenance needed by the gardeners or landscape architects? Is one of the figures a male dressed as a

Pierre-Laurent Auvray (1736-?)
after Jean Honoré Fragonard
Les Jets d'Eau, c.1779
etching

female? Later on in the book, I learned the origin of the symbolism in a sexy bedroom scene.

I don't think you have included that in the church work. Another flavour of watery symbolism, as on Hanky Panky Island.

Deeper aspects of the Minotaur story are told in the Appendix where mazes and labyrinths are discussed.

Maybe synchronicity, but we all have one place in which we store all we see – all we hear, all we taste and smell, all we think. It is the skull and it has twenty-two pieces. Two heads are better than one and you proved this with Charles Marque, so forty-four a very symbolic number. Add four to four and we get the eight of the octagon.

Another interesting thing about forty-four is that it is according to an expert at training dogs to help deaf people is that there are forty-four basic sounds, phonemes. On the architectural level, the Town Hall in the small English Town in which I live, Whitchurch has a central key stone over the entrance door with twenty-two bricks either side. The entry gap is forty-four inches wide, alluding to the two-heads-are better-than-one in public service.

Then there is something hidden, strong and flexible that supports us for our useful life or reign, our spine. It has thirty-three pieces. It is such an important symbol for Freemasons, Life of Jesus, Life of Horus and many others. In a synchronistic week, my yoga teacher Samantha Susannah told me one Tuesday she has thirty-four and later in that week on a Thursday someone else told me she had thirty-two. Most of us depend on thirty-three.

"We are hanging on to see what you have to say about our work."

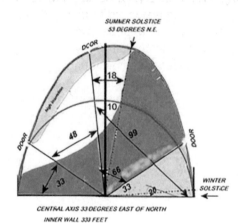

SUMMER SOLSTICE
53 DEGREES N.E.

DOOR

18

10

48

99

DOOR

DOOR

66

33

WINTER
SOLSTICE

33

20

CENTRAL AXIS 33 DEGREES EAST OF NORTH
INNER WALL 333 FEET

Well, Antoni and Christaan, you share interest in the catenary. I knew of your work in Barcelona and enjoyed many hours in Sagreda Familiale but as is so often the case, one does not learn enough. It was not until I was designing in a competition for the restoration of the Hadspen Parabola and I asked Charles Barclay about certain alignments that he said, "It is not a parabola; it is a catenary."

He also pointed out key planetary and solar alignments and I found links to the quarry where the stone came from to build the house. By analysing the word HADSPEN, I discovered a HADE is the angle of a rock deposit and the SPEN obviously alludes to suspension and the catenary which is the angle of the dangle, lots of special numbers as well.

Your amazing water lily propagating beds Bory includes a catenary.

My life is becoming fuller with connecting threads and my gathering with you, which is only happening because you

28

feel it is worth it, is maybe to do with the fact that I am still alive and possibly able to communicate with publishers, so the important attitudes you have all invested in can be spread around so the various forces of EVIL can be turned around to form LIVE.

Networking has always worked but we now have some very extensive networks and access by so many more people. Until recently, the world's biggest network was the underground mycelium of a giant fungus.

Armillaria ostoyae which penetrates 965 acres but the World Wide Web is a net catching more than any fishing net. Look at the meaning of W in the Appendix.

I think perhaps we can help serve the function of the net by better understanding and consolidating the design of our perceived realities.

All of you together have produced substantial hidden threads to do with Logic – Passion, Nature, Love and Cleverness.

What you said, Plato, namely "Everything we see is not what is coming in. It is what is projected out" is where I am now.

And how can you prove whether at this moment we are sleeping, and all our thoughts are a dream; or whether we are awake, and talking to one another in the waking state?

And you, Aristotle, said, "Eternity is a Perpetual Now."

The picture I chose of you, Plato, is linked to Lord Bath and his reaction to English Heritage when they said we could not put the Thynnehenge (Stonehenge named after Alexander Thynne) where we wanted it at Longleat. The finger is represented now by a forty feet maypole on the proposed henge site. I am reminded Randoll of the nail you were given by those restoring the ceiling in the Sistine Chapel; it was from the finger of god. Special fingernail!

I do feel honoured to be here and I suspect the later part of my journey re Hampton Court and The Kathryn of Arragon Garden; The British Rock, The Circle of Friendship and The New Stonehenge have led to your invitation see Appendix.

It is the first time I have been to such a gathering and I am what we call alive; you are dead in one sense. I am wondering if this miracle could be repeated and I can meet Gillian.

"Graham, publish the works and then progress

to the stage where you die and we will introduce you to again Gillian and my dear Camille, if not before. Time is not key. Reverse it and remove it. We EMIT time."

Thank You, Claude.

I am now going to drive home in my beloved car. Thanks to you, Flaminio, a very practical, comfortable vehicle full of symbolism.

If it had been around when you were in Paris Claude, you would have chosen it.

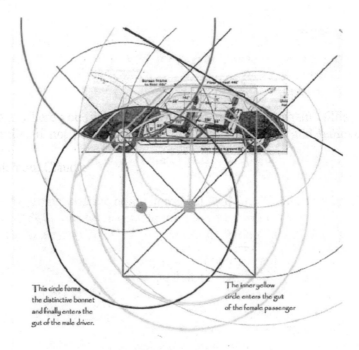

This circle forms the distinctive bonnet and finally enters the gut of the male driver.

The inner yellow circle enters the gut of the female passenger.

ANALYSIS OF DS DESIGN BY
GRAHAM BURGESS.

The Letters in
the English Alphabet

I am thinking that one of the key reasons my ghosts invited me to join them and subsequently expose some of their rebuses was because of my theory on the origins and functions of the English alphabet in uppercase. Lowercase was only introduced to extend creativity but mainly to speed up the writing process.

If you want to catch fish on a large scale, you put together a simple rectangular network of manufactured strands and key is the size of the gap between the rectangular network. If the gap is smaller than the fish you want to catch, there is a chance of your catching it. It is applied worldwide and there are around one hundred and one types of fish we seek to catch.

How you apply this network is another key factor.

A key function of the human brain is catching various external energies and then storing and mixing with others to develop a structure to help us enrich our life through communications.

The net we use is partly in our brain and it is not a simple rectilinear network but one that is quite furry with maximum opportunity for data to be held, sometimes temporarily, sometimes permanently. There is a scientific concept called tribology and this refers to the study of flows. There is an area called the boundary layer and this area around fixed elements stops the flow so whatever is in it can be better accessed. If the gaps in a fish net are bigger than the fish, then the fish escapes. In our brain gaps may form and this leads to what we call 'dementia'.

So how can we create networks to help us hold data and communicate? This book focuses on written language. A modern use of straight lines and dots is applied in bar codes now but some of the earliest written documents used a similar cleverness.

See how a simple runic pattern of straight lines in this Ogham Alphabet, linked to times of the year and special plants which were a part of everyday (and night) life.

Bar code as we apply today.

So with some simple cleverness, we constructed an alphabet based on straight lines used at various angles and curves, arched angles.

We speak English or as the French say Anglais and the angles and archangels bring us considerable benefits if applied properly in the same way an angel or archangel might help.

A question that comes up often is, "What about the other languages?"

Core to understanding is for one to understand what I mean by the 'intuit' in each letter.

It does not matter what language you speak you share in understanding basic things. Fear, high, low, big, small, funny, crazy, all mean the same thing at the simplest levels. Many of these basic intuits are understood and shared with other animals. If we shout 'sit' to a well-trained dog, it will adopt that position, so long as it is able to tune into the forty-four phonemes we apply in our communications generally. Ancient people and a few today understand what birds are saying. We all say, "A little birdie told me."

The need to communicate these intuits has led to the development of languages and in best evolutionary style this has led to variation.

A very basic level of communication is affected through bodily adjustments ranging from very slight changes in facial expression, winks, smiles and grimaces to various degrees of indication using other parts of the body, pointing or waving

Then a more sophisticated and flexible system comes into play, the oral communication. Complication begins.

As communication needed to be regularised, the use of written documents came into play and this began with simple scribing on wood or clay, often with a straight line positioned in various configurations.

The use of curved lines came next and this mixture of point, straight line and curve has evolved in many cultures with rich variation. Underlying all this variation, the intuits remain the same and I am concentrating on English because that is the language I was brought up with. Interestingly, it is proving to be highly efficient.

I keep to the uppercase as this is the simplest, the lowercase being introduced to speed up the process of writing via the introducing of more curves and linking elements.

To further get across my point, imagine a circular pond and in it the sort of filamentous algae that soon developed naturally in such places. Around it are sat people from all over the world spaced according to their nationalities.

The English-speaking person puts in a stick and twiddles it. The algae wraps round and he pulls some out and lays it before him on the flat ground. He forms the shape of a question mark. People behind him look over his shoulder and say, "What's that supposed to be?"

"It's the sign representing a question," he says. "Oh," the rest of that culture says and they go on to use it and jointly understand what it means, which intuit is being expressed.

Next to the Englishman is a Chinaman. He puts in his stick and pulls out the algae and lays it down before him in a different arrangement. The Chinese sitting behind him ask in Chinese what the shape means. He tells them in their language that it represents the questioning. "Oh," they say.

The Indian and the Arab sitting nearby do the same thing, and so the same intuit is understood using different symbols.

The Englishman notices what the Chinaman has done, so he leans over and gives a sort of questioning gesture with his hands and arms, opening his eyes and looking querulous. Eventually, he realises that the symbol the Chinaman has written means the same as the one he has written, and so different languages are learned.

Imagine that the place these people gathered had been used since time immemorial and the remains of other meetings were there. In one section a stone-age carving but since Stone Age man is dead and gone there is little opportunity for him to communicate by gesture and inference what his symbols really mean. In another section, something more recent and the pro-genitor of the Rosetta stone. Before the last analysis, no one knew the meaning of weird hieroglyphics used by the Egyptians.

It was only because they had been carved in stone adjacent to a series of symbols that were understood that we were eventually able to understand and read the Egyptian hieroglyphics.

If a particular system of symbols is practical, it is conserved and if certain symbols and their attributes have become associated they sometimes are retained in many languages. There are common denominators in the written language.

There may also be sounds that appear the same in different languages yet the shapes used to describe those intuits and sounds are different.

The relative importance of the symbols we used is determined by the value of the intuit and the frequency of their use.

There is an element of practicality in the development of the alphabet or other form of written communication and much of this is based on the potential for recreating or copying the created images easily.

In respect of the English Alphabet, the first important concept is making points. Space or, as the Greeks called it, chaos is the place we apply our skills to. We make points to start with and in the case of our written word, we choose to restrict the distance between the points by imposing parallel linear straight lines which themselves are invisible. As we insert our letters, the lines become apparent.

So from one point we progress towards another conceived point but before we start this linear journey of revelation, we decide various aspects of something we call direction. The direction we decide on is based on direction. We employ two key shapes; one is straight lines and the other is half circles. These angles and arch angles allow us to explore the mysteries as did the Angels and Archangels.

The half circles can be used with the open side facing upwards (one time), to the left (eight times), to the right (five times), downwards (not applied). The straight lines have a simple order. Vertical lines are used twenty-one times. Horizontal lines are used twelve times. Lines at an angle of forty-five degrees are used twenty-one times.

Sixty-eight options!

It is a very basic form of geometry but similar approaches have been taken exploring a wider range of angles to produce constructions of more substance and with greater variability ranging from beautiful jewellery to pyramids and stone hinges. A distance is a measure multiplied by a number.

Having adopted a configuration lines for a letter, we then seek to associate it with perceived reality. Once this is established, we can further enrich the efficiency of the alphabet by positioning letters so relative meanings can create more meaning. It is a bit like ingredients for a meal. The shorter words are the most powerful and they can be used together to enhance understanding.

Where a letter is placed in a word can be important and a classic proof of how the outthrusting format of the letter K can be employed to reinforce what a kick is. It is achieved by placing one at one end and one at the other end. The fact that the second K is facing out is irrelevant; its position hints at the power being returned when the kick impacts against something solid and the force inherent is bounced back. Same is with the word 'knock'.

The English Alphabet tunes into a key design concept: "Simplicity is the keynote of design." The most used letter in the English Alphabet is the letter E. It looks like a shelving system and that is what its intuit is. It means "capable of taking in, holding and giving out energy and information". It is a vitally useful letter and intuit. DEED, FEED, GREED, HEED, NEED, REED, SEED, SPEED, all are words where the emphasis is obvious. Multiple use, particularly in short words, easily proves this: **EVER, EVEN, EVE.**

The frequency of use varies somewhat but it is interesting to look at some of the analyses. It will vary according to topics of course.

So all you are reading is off an arrangement that is like the letter E but more shelves than in the basic letter. We only need to put three shelves in to 'get across' what concept we are accessing.

So in this store we have an upright, on the right and up, which represents the spine and then we have the horizontal lines, a lot more than three.

A simple mathematical analysis of the use of the letters in our alphabet will provide supportive clues as to their meaning.

By applying this, we can see how any NATION might benefit and begin to understand why the English Alphabet is catching on worldwide and the internet or E technology is helping.

So **E**NATION includes the six most used letters: **ETAOIN.**

E TO Z

	By letter		By frequency	
				Frequency
Letter			Letter	cy
A	1		E	0.12702
B	2		T	0.09056
C	3		A	0.08167
D	4		O	0.07507
E	5		I	0.06966
F	6		N	0.06749
G	7		S	0.06327
H	8		H	0.06094
I	9		R	0.05987
J	10		D	0.04253
K	11		L	0.04025
L	12		C	0.02782
M	13		U	0.02758
N	14		M	0.02406
O	15		W	0.0236
P	16		F	0.02228
Q	17		G	0.02015
R	18		Y	0.01974
S	19		P	0.01929

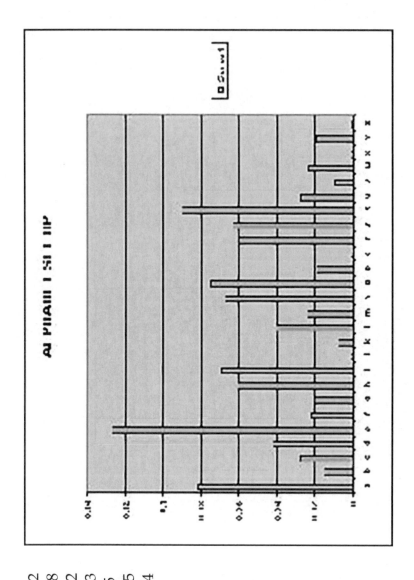

T	20	B	0.01492
U	21	V	0.00978
V	22	K	0.00772
W	23	J	0.00153
X	24	X	0.0015
Y	25	Q	0.00095
Z	26	Z	0.00074

The vowels all occur in the first half of the alphabet, the transitional *U* being at the halfway point in terms of its frequency of use.

I do believe that the refined use of the alphabet has led to letters finding special relative positions whatever message is being compiled. If we accept this, then maybe we can ask why any letter is where it is in the layout of the alphabet. Before we start to look at the intuits, we should look at the very simple construction method used for the letters in uppercase. They are all made from a mixture of straight lines and half circles.

Letter		
A	3	0
B	1	2
C		1
D	1	1
E	4	
F	3	
G	2	1
H	3	
I	1	
J	1	1
K	3	
L	2	
M	4	
N	3	
O		2
P	1	1
Q	1	2
R	2	1
S		2
T	2	
U	2	1
V	2	
W	4	

X	2
Y	3
Z	3
	53 15
	68

Another two things to feed into your mind-set before we go any further is that we have chosen to write script within parallel lines so as to speed up writing and printing. Size is measure times a number.

The late Leonard Schlain in his book The Alphabet against the Goddess postulates that all the cultures that have adopted this style of script have eliminated the Goddess or feminine side from their thinking. It is left-hand brain thinking.

The other thing is that we should not be limited by the standard direction of a letter in a word. In some cases, we accept the intuit working in a reverse direction but for case of writing, we write it as if it is left to right. We do not just read left to write; a whole word is a picture. There is a common proof of this:

Did you konw you're a guiens? Jsut the fcat taht you can atllacuy raed tihs psot porves taht fcat. The huamn mnid is so pufowerl; it can dcodee tihs txet eevn tguohh eervy sglnie wrod is slepled iocenrtclry. The one cavaet is taht the frist and lsat lertets are pervresed in erevy wrod. Cidrgbame Uitesirnvy cetoudncd a sduty and fnuod taht the biarn deos not raed eevry snlige lteetr, but wodrs as a wohle.

The fact that we can read as a picture does not prevent us positioning letters in creative ways as we will see later. A separate skill was the creation of clever shuffling to create codes such as The Caesars Code and Pigpen Cipher.

The filtering to find meanings can be applied on many levels and a key part of this publication is to do with Hebrew focus PARADISE, THE SECRET GARDEN. No vowels in ancient Hebrew so PRDS. *P* is Pradash (surface meaning). *R* is Remez (hint of something below the surface). *D* is Drasha (allegorical story not to be taken literally); *S* is SOD (secret).

So look at the words and the letters and seek the REMEZ.

So dear GHOSTS, you are well-done hosts and this focus on your current being has helped me deal with the loss of one of the best hosts in my life, Gillian.

The name has ILLI in the middle as has trillion, million, billion and filling.

The Letter *A*

So let us see what we can do with our alphabet starting with the letter *A*.

The letter *A* is the third most used letter. It stands like a very firm construction at the front end of the alphabet. Part of its meaning is communicated through the angle formed by the uprights. In the same way when one rises from bed, one positions the legs at a useful angle and in the same way we encompass a desirable distance with a pair of compasses when we begin to design something. The key thing is acceptable parameters within our perceived reality. It is a well-balanced approach.

The creation of this shape allows us to focus on whatever is within the parameters yet to see the exterior to some degree and accept it.

Most of our life is experienced at the lower levels and whilst above us there is a spire, to which we may aspire. We do tend to spend most of our useful lives low down. Capability Brown said that no one looks above twenty-seven degrees unless there is a special reason. The angle for picking on modern shop shelves is affected by this. If one goes out of the top of the spire, one enters what the Greeks called chaos or space. It's not necessarily negative. We prefer to stay away from that in everyday life, so the symmetrical *A* stands as a statement that we are going to move forward into our alphabet.

If we want to define the existence of anything, we can say, "There is *A*" whatever it is.

Wherever the *A* appears, it intuits 'of substance in this accepted reality'.

It is at the beginning of much of what you have done dear hosts. **ART.**

It is rarely used in pairs because its inherent individual meaning almost covers every eventuality.

In the exception, **AAH** implies some sort of surprise in the volume of reality extant at the moment. See later how the letter *H* is connected with the letter *A*.

The Letter *B*

Second in Alphabet and 20th most used:

We have to consider the *A* as being a shape that encloses us and all we perceive. It's only when we come to the letter *B* that we begin to insert an image of ourselves in the design of the letter. We take our place.

It is the simple vertical stroke of the *I*.

Having established this on the left-hand side, we move to the right to create the next part of the intuit of *B* and this is two half circles firmly fixed to the upright. The semi-circle is a shape we create and if we continue with it, we eventually meet up where we started and there we have created a perfect circle and the letter *O*. As you will later see, the intuit in *O* is birthing.

The two half circles hint at the fact that we have positively ceased the creative act of circling at a chosen point in order to fix whatever has been created against the upright and we have introduced the concept of plenitude by doing it twice. It is important that the double application may mean a lot more than double but the design seeks to minimise use of line and space to get across the message.

The fixed sort of ancestral value in a more focussed and simpler way leads to our using one half circle as in DID or as in DADDY. It is creativity retained securely for future use.

One should always relate this intuit to the intuits in adjacent letters as sometimes a letter is used in a particular relevant position to encourage us to question whether how that intuit is disposed in the current reality. **DEAD, DEATH, DUD and DIP,** all give hints as to the comparative meanings of all the letters and their intuits.

The fact that we have two of these in the letter *B* suggests plenitude and a high degree of potentially useful energy safely stored there.

The curved bits push out and in one word which has three of the letters in it, **BUBBLE,** the intuit is made very clear. There is a certain amount of flexibility but it is temporarily secure. Its fulsome nature is manifest in words like **BOOBS** and **BUM.** In fact those parts of the anatomy look a bit like *B*s.

To Be or not to Be, that is the question.

The words **Bible** and **Boebel** are used to describe a **b**ook full of all sorts of things and by definition full of variability and possibly benefits.

The Letter *C*

Third in the alphabet and 12th most used:

From the simple concept of one point reaching to another point in a straight line, we see one of the most creative acts ever. The line curves and we begin to form the circle, the arch angle.

We do not complete this circle but leave space for something else to occupy it in the future. This is the safe context for future creativity. On one side, in this case the left-hand side, we have protection but the right side, the right-hand side is open for things to enter and leave.

Its power is not just emanating from itself, as eleven other letters in the alphabet employ its symbology in their structure.

Eight creative c-shaped curves have their external curved boundary on the east, five in the west, one in the south and none in the north.

The word CAN provides a powerful basis for anything in our reality, hence the *C* preceding the *A*.

A CASE or another CAN holds things with some potential for the future.

CAKES get cut up, hence the outward thrusting *K*.

A CACHE has two *C*s and a cache is full of something. A CACKLE is a series of noises full of noise.

So the *C* has an intuit of 'capable of creation'.

If we look for a word that has two combined with three birthing *O*s, we see this intuit fully explored.

COCOON:

Two *C*s for capable of creation and three *O*s for birthing. Birthing of what? The *N* poses that question. See later: *N*.

Words beginning with *C* are the third greatest in number, only exceeded by *P* and *S*.

The Letter *D*

We alluded to the meaning earlier and it is to do with hereditary substance. So a 'capable of creation' *C* is sealed off for future use.

It often appears at the end of words to substantiate a positive belief in an acceptable end result. GOOD, FOOD, BREAD, BRED, FED, LED and SAID.

It provides substance at the beginning of words: DEAR, DATE, DEAL, DIVE, DRIVE, DOOR, DEEP and DIVINE.

The word **DID** is a very strong proof of this intuit.

Three in a word emphasise the presence of creative potential

DECIDED, DIVIDED, DEDICATED and ADDICTED
Addicted hints at energies of *D* intensely linked, same *D* repeating.

DREADED has three and that alludes to a greater amount of substance perhaps imminent and empowered by the intense external energy of the *R*.

The word DEAD intuits as something that is in part sealed off from the rest of reality.

DO, see later the birthing *O*.

A word that alludes to establishing something in the future

At the beginning of a regular part of our lives, the word **DAY**

DEED IS ENERGY AND INFORMATION CAPACITY FIRMLY HELD.
In the word GOD, it alludes to the powerful energies derived from the previous two letters being available for on-going use.

The Letter *E*

What an obvious design this is! It is a shelving system with shelves coming out from an upright on the left and like a mini-warehouse. The intuit in it is **'capable of taking in holding and giving out energy and information'.**

Where we wish to imply more in a word, we put in two of these symbols and double the intuit energy.

DEED, FEED, GREED, HEED, NEED, REED, SEED, WEED and EXCEED

WETTER, BETTER, CLEANER, BEDDED, SEEDED, SEEN and BEEN

It is high value as an intuit and that is perhaps why the symbol feeding it is the most used letter in our alphabet. It far exceeds the other letters.

Where it appears at the end of a word, one should consider which way the shelf is facing. Often it should be recognised as facing back into the word as it has a conserving value.

FLEE, FREE, BEE, SEE and TREE, all have out reaching components but when it is a lone *E* on the end of a letter, then maybe we apply a more conservative approach to the energy and information exchange.

ANYWHERE, SPARE, BARE, RARE, FLARE, CARE and SNARE, all intuit a more controlled use of *E*.

Lately we use *EBAY*, a gathering place, not of water but information.

Three horizontal lines are enough to get across the 'shelving intuit' but a book is based on the same geometry. A book has an upright on the left and each page has more than one shelf to hold the letters which make up the words. This is on the 25th shelf on this page.

When we first look into a book, we turn the pages from back to front and then stop at a PAGE. Read backwards. It is the EGAP which may release the information.

A key tool we use is called our EYE.

The Letter *F*
Sixteenth most used letter
Sixth in alphabet

Well, it is a bit like the *E* but without that lower shelf. This might imply that there is a little less balance and uniformity and balance in respect of energy and information being exchanged. Not so secure in foundations.

Question the shelf capacity.

There is a sense of doubt or **IFFYNESS.**

The simple word IF is proof. The *I* is the definitive instance of individuality.

The *F* focuses one's attention on the need to find out what is not quite what one might expect.

Facades and faces are what you see on the surface but what is beyond.

A facet is only a small part of something and a factor is again only one part, what else? Bright is obvious but what does **fade** imply.

How **far** is far? **Falcons** are far **off** often, flying on their feathers. Falling is full of unknowns. Falsity may be hinted at in fables but that does not mean they cannot be fun. Fantasia can be a frivolous place to be.

Fear involves unknown forces and a feast is where you cannot be quite sure of what is available to eat.

Feeding and feeling all start with the iffyness incentive and hopefully it leads to a good end result. Once you have tried and tested an activity with the scrutiny of iffyness and you have resolved that it is probably not too much of a problem, you can proceed. It need not be dangerous. That's how you find things, refine things.

A most useful **finder of rabbits is a ferret.**

Sometimes you do fail and then you have a fiasco.

Fish are very difficult to find and the metaphor for fishing is much used. See later for **FIN.**

We are fed most by something that comes each day from the EAST.

The Letter *G*

The seventh most used letter and seventh in the alphabet, very harmonic. It means 'well done'.

The is a letter made up of two letters, the *C* and the *T* combined.

The letter *C* as we have explained is 'capable of creation' and on its own there is scope for more creation.

If however one locks up any further creation by putting in place the letter *T*, we establish a fixed point in time and a very substantial one.

The letter *T* **intuits 'of substance in this reality'.** I may tell you to a *T*.

It allows one to appraise the creativity and the statement that it is substantial.

It has become a Masonic brand name image for the Great Architect. It appears at the beginning of **GOD. GOD,** if invested in positively, leads to **GOOD.**

To return to fishing, we have a word associated very much with iffyness and a device that actually looks like a *G*, a **GAFF**. A gaff is used to land large fish. Another key item that ensures on-going substance in life was the stick used to control cattle, a **GOAD. The goad became a powerful Egyptian symbol and also became basis of many measures. Key animal: a GOAT.**

GAG securely locks things in this existence as perceived. (See earlier *A*.)

The letter can be associated with all sorts of consolidated things and the *G* may be associated with positive or negative. The key thing is that it represents something substantial.

AN**G**ER made permanent by putting a *D* in front becomes DAN**G**ER. Put a nurturing *M* in front (see later) and we have a positive result possibly. MANGER. Various good people started in mangers.

A **G**AP is OK but you do need to know it is there if it is substantial. MIND THE GAP.

KEY IS THE QUESTION WHAT SORT OF SUBSTANCE IS IMPLIED BY THE *G*.

Think about GAGGLE, GIGGLE and GOGGLE.

DOG alludes to something that has hereditary substance and by giving birth to things gives a sense of being well done.

A very clear clue is in the word **EGG**.

The Letter *H*

This is eighth used and not surprising because it has long been associated with the UNIVERSAL ASPIRANT. It is also eighth in alphabet and a very lucky number to the Chinese. Key is: one takes in air, holds it and then releases it.

It is very lively. *I* for the male, *H* for the breath, *O* for the female and *H* for the breath, **IHOH** an old spelling of JEHOVA.

Repeat it and life goes on IHOHIOHIOHIOH.

Attract attention to your living self by shouting **HI.**

HA is an expression of initial being.

It also has the intuit of being important in itself but dependent on some repetition. HALF and HAVE allude to the potential for more.

HAMMERS, HANDS and HAMPERS.

HELLOH occurs when someone embraces ELLO in the offering of shared breath.

HELL you have to watch. It is potentially dangerous but HELLO is fine. When two people say Hello, two opportunities to exchange life experiences (*H*) two opportunities to give, hold and take in information (*E*), four opportunities to exchange life energies (*L*) and two opportunities to give birth to something (*O*).

HELP includes the *P* to indicate some external outreach is needed.

There is an exaggerated element of aspiration in HIGH.

Be correct or RIGHT.

H is to do with holding.

The *H* is an *A* with the top opened up to allow passage of 'perceived reality'.

The Letter *I*

Ninth letter in alphabet and fifth most used:

This shape is one of the simplest marks man can make. It is easily done and easily understood. It was used as a measure and then became the key shape in many scripts including our alphabet.

It is one straight line and it also refers to the number one. We use the word ONE to refer to *I*.

WHAT DOES ONE THINK?

It starts from one point and ends simply in another at the end of a straight line.

It refers to ACCEPTED SELF REALITY IN PLACE.

In words, it provides instance and a focus of reflection. In itself it is very balanced.

Its upright rigidity led to association with the male phallus and maleness: RIGS and RICKS

Columns supported lintels and arches: ANGLES AND ARCHANGLES

The fact that it has accepted ends does introduce the important aspect of our logic system and that is considerable ignoring of the fact that reality is only what we make it.

The straight line was the basis of early building and landscape. It is a very practical shape to use. The straight line and regular perimeter forming geometries were the basis of landscape design until Hogarth's Line of Perfect Beauty was introduced. After this, a more natural line was adopted.

Some other languages use such shapes but not our English alphabet. It is all straight lines and, with a few exceptions, half circles.

A very clear indication of its meaning can be derived from the word **IT**. See later.

The Letter *J*

The tenth letter in the alphabet but twenty-two letters are used more than *J* and it is a component of relatively few words. This is not surprising when one considers its intuit. You do not want an intuit as unstable as *J* playing a key part in your life.

Its intuit is **"something that is fluid, is temporarily restricted, but will soon be released".**

MATURE FRUIT WAITS ON A TREE. One seeks to make some JAM. First one squeezes the fruit. JUICE emerges. We wish to temporarily restrict that JUICE until we serve it up in glasses so we put it into a JUG. The remaining fruit is made into JAM and put in a container, only temporarily as it will be released when we come to eat it. This is a JAR.

The Egyptians put chosen pieces of the human body after death into containers, to be released into a later existence, canopic JARS.

Having taken the jam home, a burglar raids the district. He is a jam burglar. He breaks into your home using a rigid piece of metal that he places in a chosen position and applies pressure, temporarily, until access is gained .The JEMMY is forced into the place either side of a door, through which you enter. It is the place where you are temporarily restricted but from which you are released when you are inside the JAMBS and overhead a JOIST.

He steals your jam and the next morning the police follow a trail of dripped jam to his home. There he has transferred all the jam from jam jars into a larger container, temporarily, a JERRY CAN.

He is arrested and twelve people are gathered temporarily, the JURY. The evidence is brought together and if jury FINDS HIM GUILTY, a man, called a JUDGE, releases a judgement and the man is sent to a place where he will be temporarily restricted but will be released, JAIL or JUG.

JETS, whether they be water or aircraft, depend on temporary restriction and release.

JUMPING, JESTING, JIVING and JOY, all are temporary.

IESU became JESUS as this symbolic figure went through a transitional stage.

A spear is one thing and sometimes you let go of it, but sometimes you hold onto it and poke people, not so a JAVELIN.

Most of us now drive cars that move smoothly and regularly without any temporary impediment but watch out for JALOPYS, a lot of stop and start.

Seasonal release is hinted at as JANUARY comes half way through the year and JUNE and JULY signal a mid-summer shift.

The Letter *K*

Eleventh most used as a letter but words beginning with *K* are very low in frequency.

This is because its intuit is to do with relative direction of outwardly bursting forces.

Yes, we have the firm *I*, but then there are lines radiating out in a very dramatic way, in a way unique to the letter *K*.

It may sound like the letter *C* but it has none of the flexible embracing creativity.

It intuits out-thrusting.

It is one letter that can reveal what was said earlier that a letter can carry a message flavoured by its position.

If we take the word **K**ICK, we see the outward thrust of the first *K*. The force emanates from the *I* and with open energy, the *C* expands. So far it is not an effective kick. Only when that which has been the focus of the swing comes into contact and the force is blocked and sent back do we get KIC**K**.

Accumulations of things dispersed do not return until they come BAC**K**.

The outgoing force can be subtle and of high value: **K**ISS, **K**INDNESS.

It can be very significant: **K**ILL. The underlying energy of the *L* is kicked out.

If we allude to something we take in as part of nurturing, we use the word **MILK.**

The Letter *L*

The eleventh most used letter in the alphabet, twelfth in the alphabet and a letter at the beginning of many words:

It is used as a start to a substantial number of words.

The intuit is **"intense energy of an emotional/spiritual sort and often underlying"**.

The symbol is there to focus you on the power of the energy which can be good or bad so as to perhaps facilitate some effective management of that energy. One might accept the letter in certain contexts or try to control that energy.

If I am **WELL**, that's pretty OK. In fact it is more than OK. It is great. If I am **ILL**, something needs to be done.

HELL, you have to be wary of as it tends to lead to horrible things. If you put an *O* for birthing on the end that is good, all the inherent energies in the word will lead to something.

H the breath of life; *E* the exchange of energy and information and two emotional and spiritual energies out of our control, *O* birthing. As two people greet each other, we have all those letters doubled: **HELLO HELLO**. Two breaths, two opportunities to give out take in and store energy and information; four opportunities to exchange emotional energies and two opportunities for birthing. Wonderful!

Strike a piece of suitably shaped metal a BELL and energy will escape in all directions, very much uncontrolled.

SWELL also hints at expansion of a somewhat uncontrolled sort.

FELL is an iffy focus of directional energy.

Whilst it refers to emotional and spiritual energies, it clearly refers to results that are very apparent and understood. That is why it works as a signal of power.

The word WILL is proof of the fact that whilst *W* is full of unknowns the word ends with energies as yet undefined but manifest as a commitment to achieving something.

Double *L*s hint at extremes always.

ALL, BALL, CALL, FALL, GALL, HALL, MALL, PALL, TALL, WALL
BELL, CELL, DELL, FELL, HELL, NELL, PELL, MELL, SELL, TELL, WELL

ILL, BILL, FILL, HILL, KILL, MILL, PILL, RILL, SILL, SPILL, THRILL, TILL, WILL

ROLL, TOLL, BULL, CULL, DULL, FULL, GULL, HULL, LULL, MULL, NULL, PULL, ALLOW, SHALLOW, FALLOW, FOLLOW and HOLLOW.

The best example I know of the *L* energy streaming is in the word: PARALLEL.

Three *L* s. The two *A*s form a very substantial perceived reality. The *R* provides one sort of energy, very controlled in this case, locked in between our two perceived realities, the *A*s but then the *L*s stream out focussed by the outreaching arms of the *E*.

The Letter *M*

It is the thirteenth letter in the alphabet and fourteenth most used letter but at the beginning of many words, in fact the fourth most popular word starter.

It is central in its position and number of uses but in recognition of its function a common starter.

The intuit is **nurturing and worthy of retention.**

A very common utterance is made when someone says something which you hear and which you decide to take in with care interest for future consideration. It is three *M*s in a row: **MMM.**

It manifests in other nurturing words like MA, MUM or MAM.

The Egyptians carefully wrapped bodies into MUMMIES and MUMMY is a three-letter emphasis of nurturing.

Nurturing is to do with putting energy and care into something but without one really being sure of the outcome. This is what happens when one brings up children or creates a garden.

Measured input with definite forecast-able outcomes is not nurturing; it is curatorship.

HAMMERS only work if they are controlled carefully.

A lot of very important words begin with MA which intuits "nurturing in this accepted reality".

The word MAD seeks to focus one's attention on the fact that special nurturing is necessary.

MADE is where the *E* holds useful energies in association.

MAN alludes to stability and caring but with the *N* alluding to his intellectual energy.

MAP alludes to careful substance somewhat spread about. You will discover about the real substance of a MAT later.

The Letter *N*

This is the fourteenth letter in the alphabet but the sixth most used.

The intuit is **"test all assumptions"**.

It brings a sense of CHANGING to many words.

In one culture, it was associated with fish. When a fish suddenly changes its direction, it makes an *N* shape and the part of its body used to achieve this is the word that starts with the iffy *F* and ends with *N*: **FIN**.

Chartres cathedral is based on Fishy Geometry. You do not enter the underlying body of the church until you have followed the symbolic maze to its centre where you finish. This is at the end of the fin in the design.

Another word that has a sense of "where are we?" is 'finish'. 'Finished' is more definite and the *D* provides that substance.

There is much more doubt in the word BEGINNING, so it has three.

OPENING has two, so it is not so unknown.

The birthing *O* (see next letter) placed before *N* really does give birth to something.

ON AND ON AND ON AND ON UNTIL ONE IS DONE.

It allows CONTINUITY, hints at something more remote like INFINITY.

The extreme negative is expressed by putting the *N* in front of the supreme positive of birthing *O*: **NO**.

It can be personalised when one says **NO ONE**.

NO and ON are opposite in meaning and letter disposition.

Do you want me to carry ON or NOt?

The Letter *O*

Fourth most used and a very positive intuit:

We have seen how the letter *C* is "capable of creation". Well, if we continue with the circumference of that *C* as far as we can go, we complete the creation and create a letter *O*.

That *O* is then ready to give birth and it retains its shape as birthing takes place.

The intuit is "capable of creation".

If you want to intuit more of a thing, put two together in a word.

FOOD, GOOD, HOOD, MOOD, LOOK, BOOK, COOK, HOOK, TOOK, HOOT, LOOT, ROOT, FOOL, POOL, TOOL, ROOM, BOOM, DOOM, LOOM, WOOD and ZOO
COCCOON: 3 *C*s and 3 *O*s

It hints at substance even when only one appears in a word.

BOB, COB, FOB, GOB, HOB, JOB, LOB, MOB, NOB, ROB, SOB, YOB
BOG, BOW

SO and then what next? **GO** where **TO**?

TOO many implies rather more than one would ideally want.

A **LOT** is a lot but **LOOT** hints at more.

The Letter *P*

It is the nineteenth most used letter and fifteenth in the alphabet:

This letter consists of an upright straight letter *I* referring to the self-reality in place and then a curved line that is like a *C* in reverse pointing out to the right.

It hints at something swelling and maybe reaching out for a bit…

The word **POP** intuits something being born in an explosive way. We just **POP** down to the **SHOP** or the **PUB.**

PAPER has facilitated the spread of words all over the world and **PEPPER** has three for very obvious reasons.

PARAPETS are right near the edge.

The intuit is hinted at but the opposite suggested in the word **STOP.**

It is used to help us understand that not being stable can be a bit tricky, so we avoid **POPPING OUT** all the time.

It is generally good energy. **PUPILS** of all sorts and some of the **POPES** are **POPULAR.**

The word **SLEEP** shows how the intuit of the *P* reflects on the extreme energy intuited by the two *E*s. Like **DEEP AND STEEP,** THERE IS A HINT OF EXTREMITY.

The Letter *Q*
Seventeenth in Alphabet and twenty-fifth most Used

This letter looks like a letter O but whilst O is fourth most used due to its creativity, *Q* is the twenty-fifth because it has little inherent from anything of its own.

The clear statement of birthing the very important symbolism of *O* is interrupted by a line which leads one to ask 'why'.

It hints at unknowns: QUAKE, QUEST, QUESTION, QUERY, QUELLE and QUOTA.

So what is going to become?

There is some acceptance that the use of this letter will lead to something else, so it occurs almost every time at the beginning of words with the letter *U* which intuits at transition. Proof is in the word QUEUE.

The Letter *R*
Eighteenth in Alphabet and Ninth most Used

It intuits "intense external energy". This is not the same as the spiritual or emotional energies associated with the letter *L*.

A classic example is the sun. There is a circle and emanating from it an infinite number of lines. No time to write them all, so we pick two and this forms the letter *R*.

The relationship between the sun and our perceived reality was used by the Egyptians when they created the symbol **RA.**

Add some 'substance in this reality' *T* and we have ART.

This inherent energy is hinted at when the *R* is used more than once.

TERROR, HORROR, ERROR, TERRIER, WHIRR
Looking into a MIRROR results in energy going to and fro.

RRR goes the motorbike rushing by or the Tiger **ROARING.**

An example of how the intuit is there to focus one's attention on the measure of *R* is revealed in **RARER.**

The creative *C* and ARE lead to the very good CARE applied by a CARER.

ANGER is a powerful energy and ideally we should control it. If we invest substance *D* in it, we expose ourselves to **DANGER**. Put an *M* of nurturing in front of it and we have a place where energy can result in positive end: a **MANGER.**

If we bring the other sort of energy, the more spiritual and emotional energy into the word **ANGER** and replace the *R* with *L*, **ANGER BECOMES ANGEL**.

There is another word which is full of both sorts of energy and that is **PARALLEL.**

Yes, it is an out-thrusting word, hence the *P* at the beginning. The first external energy is firmly locked between two stable *A*s. From that part of the word, it evolves with the energies outside of our control the *L*s being launched. The next *E* refers to the on-going taking in holding and giving out that same energy structure and it continues to the end of the word and beyond.

The Letter *S*

Nineteenth in the alphabet but eighth most used:

It intuits "of living substance in this reality".

To be: in English IS, French EST, German IST and Spanish ESSTE.

If you want a word to be fleshier, put two in.

HISS, KISS, CARESS

Involve more than normal and have a **SESSION.**

Could last longer than a PROCESSION

Being involves sensibility, so we have the concept of DEPRESSION.

The concept PRESS is used a lot: IMPRESS, DEPRESS, SUPRESS and COMPRESS.

SSSSHHHH, go to SLEEP.

Immortal symbolic words like IO, IUNO, IUPATER, all gods without flesh and without the letter that signifies that, the *S* links to our sharing as mortals.

Put the *S* in the middle of IU and you have ISU.

A god of the flesh or living god. ISLAM is full of spiritual nurturing.

Human beings are full of moisture, so the *S* carries that intuit.

SLOSHING ABOUT IN THE SLUSH IS LUSCIOUS.

The Letter *T*

Here's a letter *I* with another one balanced across the top in a firm sort of way. It is second most used, so it is a foundation. It is twentieth in the alphabet.

The intuit is "of substance in this reality".

Tell me to a *T* we say.

Having started by initiating an accepted reality with the letter *A*, the placing of the *T* after it is very substantiating: AT. Bring in the creative *C* and we have **ACT**. **IT establishes our substance.**

If living substance *S* comes into the scene, it may **SIT**.

If you sit as the *I* and look one way and see the enormous substance offered by *B* but you are between that and the *T* at the other end of the word, you are in the realms of **BIT.**

A small creature of substance approaches and it is capable of birthing as proven by the *O* in the middle. **TOT**s are full of substantial future promise.

Rubbish is thrown away but some things are kept within our perceived reality *A*. We call it **TAT**.

TAT starts as something someone does not really want to keep but they do not want to throw it away. They want to keep it in the system. So it is given free to a special sort of a shop where the prices are so low that someone will probably buy the object and take it back into their accepted reality. People who shop in such places hardly ever visit with a plan of what they might buy because they have no idea what is flowing in the stream of TAT.

Everywhere it is used it brings strength and substance intuits. In some cases, it reminds us of extremes in various directions.

A **PAT** is not extreme but it is firm in a minor way. More substantial uses **BAT, CAT, FAT, HAT, MAT, RAT, SAT and VAT**

Bring the iffyness of *F* **in and you have FIT.**

I have said *L* is intense energy of the sort one cannot control completely so LIT.

TALL is very extreme.

The bursting out of *P* is appropriately at the end of **TAP.**

As with so many letters, double use relates to emphasis of the intuit.

ATTACK, ATTRITION, ATTRACT, ATTENTION,

ATTEND, ATTITUDE, ATTEST, ATTRIBUTE, ATTACH,

ATTAIN, ATTEMPT, ATTENUATE, ATTUNE and ATTRACT

The Letter *U*

It is thirteenth most used and it is actually half-way through the alphabet. Well-positioned.

The intuit in *U* is **TRANSITIONAL.**

So many words begin with UN and it infers that maybe the opposite to what the second half of the word means is actually what is extant.

If one looks at short words, we see the intuit more clearly.

USE: The *U* relates to energies and information in movement in respect of 'beings of substance'.

UP hints at the change as one leaps away from the *I* with the *P*.

UPPITY more so.

UNDER: Very similar to **UPPER** but you cannot sense as much easily so the 'test all assumptions'. *N* is in there but a *D* of established substance keeps us lower rather than higher.

UDDER: well and truly Underneath and a transitional thing.

UMBRELLA

The word **USUAL** has no negative intuits. It alludes to possible underlying creativity. A letter *U* is a *C* containing.

HURRY, RUSH, PUSH, CRUSH and RUNNING

As *S*s we are exposed to something that we really cannot encompass with our understanding **SUN.**

Key part of a boat is the **HULL.**

The Letter *V*

It is twenty-second in the alphabet and twenty-third most used.

It has powers of transformation, hinting at relative values.

EVE allows all energies to transcend.

EVEN implies "testing that assumption in some way" because the *N* is in there.

EVERY more external energy promised from the *R* and a *Y* at the end that hints at future beneficence (see later).

VALVE hints at change of flow.
FLAVOUR subtle tastes.
LOVE, LIVE, ALIVE
LOVE LEADS TO EVOLVE if read backwards repeatedly.
LIVE REVERSED IS EVIL.
MORE SUBSTANTIAL CONSERVED EVIL IS DEVIL.
VERGE, VACILLATE, VOYAGE, VISTA and VIEW, all have edges.
A VIRUS has intense energies *R* which can enter into US.

A very well-balanced state is LEVEL, all those external emotional and spiritual energies held in balance.

The Letter *W*

It is the twenty-third letter in the alphabet and the fifteenth most used. We are an enquiring species.

This use factor must be changing as the www comes into play worldwide.

The intuit is: "We are not quite sure what follows this symbol."

Geometrically, it is full of 'change of directions and conditions'.

It does not enclose anything.

In our search for more information on key issues, we use words that start with it.

WHO, WHY, WHERE, WHEN, WHY, WHAT, WHICH, WILL, WHETHER
WAND, WANGLE, WONKY, WANTON, WHIM
WHEEL, WHIRL, WHISK, WHIZZ
WHO?

In front of the intense external energies *R* bearing down on our accepted reality *A*, we have **WAR.**

WARM, WASH,
WAVE

The transitional *V* is in there.

With 'taking in, holding and giving out energy and information', *E* and in a very prolific outgoing way, *B*, we have **WEB.**

The two *L*s of intense spiritual and emotional energy *L* near to the in-gathering *E* and preceded with *W* offers great promise. **WELL.**

The simplest proof? Go into a crowded room and shout a three-letter word with a birthing *O* in the middle and a *W* at either end.

Everyone will look round to see what is happening that they do not know about.

WOW!

The Letter *X*

Twenty-fourth in the Alphabet and Twenty-fourth most Used:

It is exceptional. If we had a language that used this letter or intuit a lot, it would have little stable substance and we would not be able to **RELAX**.

TAX can be **TAXING** as it is something that comes out of nowhere. Forces that maybe unexpected emerge.

SEX, MIX, VEX

One might be able to **FIX** them, of course.

TOXIC is an *X* lying between the substance of this reality *T* and 'capable of creation' *C* at the end.

OX is powerful and productive even as a beast.

To contain more of anything, put all of it with *B*, in a **BOX**.

Suitably formed **EXCESSES** can be deemed **EXCELLENT**.

So having established those letters that service most of the useful intuits, we are nearing the end. The *X* hints at that but allows us to consider that whatever has been intuited before there may be differences, so the intuit is: "Keep your mind open. Do not be complacent."

A classic example of letter shape and meaning tuning into product design is **OXO**. The two *O*s represent eyes looking at you. The word is doubly palindromic. It is coloured brown to represent the earth and it is in a shape associated with sound construction, a cube. The size echoes the space needed to pick with your fingers and the cube is covered with a hint at very sound construction, steel. It is covered in metal foil. Red and white are key colours in the human psyche, blood and sperm.

OMO applied a similar approach but not so comprehensive.

The Letter Y

Is eighteenth most used and twenty-fifth in the alphabet. What an interesting comparison! Right at the end, yet used a lot!

ISIS, the Egyptian symbol of total creativity, had a number and it was eighteen.

Another eighteen, the first oxygen on Earth was O18, not O2 as now but it gave rise to all life.

The letter *Y* is like a simple tree. The arms reach up and the intuit is clear.

Y means "capable of taking in, holding energy and information for future beneficent use".

Put the A of our accepted reality in front of it.

BAY, DAY, GAY, HAY, JAY, LAY, MAY, PAY, RAY, SAY, WAY, PRAY and TRAY, All words full of promise.

LIBRARY?

M IS NURTURING, so saying something MAY happen does show some faith in the intuit of nurturing and persisting.

MAY is the name that in pre-calendrical times hinted at so much life and growth to come after the winter.

In Sanskrit, MAY meant little points. It alluded to the little points of green leaves and their potential to grow to full size, bringing extra provender and, producing from the CO2, lots of O18.

NE'ER CAST YOUR CLOUT TILL ALL THOSE LITTLE LEAVES ARE FULLY OUT (SUMMER).

A very good example of something that takes in energy and information that has been processed by two *E*s is EYE.

The Letter *Z*

Twenty-sixth Letter in the Alphabet and Twenty-sixth most Used:

There is a sense of finality but only in the sense of this alphabet. It is still a real shape, so it is not extinct. It intuits at "being outside the accepted norm".

ZIG ZAG is not in line.

LAZE is an end thing.

LAZY hints at not gathering in and holding things for future beneficent use.

GAZE is a sort of vague look.

MAZE is a modern word and the *Z* hints at getting lost.

SQUEEZE is press to an indeterminate shape.

SNEEZE implies an outward, uncontrolled, unexpected breath.

BREEZE is neither still nor windy.

FREEZE stops you going in a solid sort of way.

DRIZZLE is half-hearted rain.

FIZZLE is the tired end of BLAZES.

I did say MAZE is a **new use** of the letter **Z**.

This is because **there used to be a twenty-seventh letter of the alphabet**.

It was a symbol that looked a bit like the letter *Z*.

It was **pronounced like the letter *Y*** and I think it was a very optimistic symbol to say, **"The end result of employing this set of letters will be to bring future beneficent use."**

There was a twenty-seventh letter, the ampersand.

AARON	Great source of energy for distribution to many
ABEL	Sound and promoter of emotional realities
ABNER	Sound advocate of testing life forces.
ABRAHAM	Puts lots of energy into caring for the world we live in.
ADA	Of established being in this reality, a solid balanced person
ADAIR	Sound and very energetic in an individual way
ADAH	established and lively person
ADAM	Established, balanced and conserving good things for humanity
ADELAIDE	Very sound communicator of spiritual feelings
ADELINE	Very sound and with sensitive and good direction
ADRIAN	Secure with a creative and exploratory mind
ADRIENNE	Sound with outreaching attitude to learning about new things
AGATHA	Extremely sound, secure and full of life
AGNES	Sound and self-critical
AILEEN	Sound but open to tantalising stimuli
AMY	Sound and nurturing person
ALAN	Has well-established emotions with sensitivity to outside factors
ALBERT	Emotional and creative, capable of creating productive set-ups
ALETHEA	Makes the most of life by productive communal effort
ALEXANDRA	Reliable and productive practical worker and leader
ALEXIS	Outside the mainstream and passionate
ALFRED	Sound, spiritual connecting with mysterious forces to good established ends
ALGERNON	Sound, spiritual and very energetic, may discover new things
ALICE	Sound, spiritual and creative
ALISON	Having a strong sensitive presence
ALMA	Very sensitive and secure mother
ALTHEA	Sound and spiritually firm, socially creative

AMANDA	Nurturing and caring for all in many ways
AMARYLLIS	Nurturing to bring intense emotional benefits for the future
AMBER	Nurturing and capable of generating stimulus to others
AMBROSE	Takes care of external sources of energy
AMELIA	Balanced person, capable of nurturing spiritual things
AMY	Great storehouse of caring attributes
ANNABELLA	Promotes and cares for new emotional energies
ANDREW	Very energetic with tantalising objectives
ANGELA	Substantial, questioning sound person with emotional sensitivities
ANN	Competent but also adventurous
ANNA	Surprisingly caring for everyone and adventurous
ANNETTE	Very analytical and caring and bringer of stability and substance
ANTHEA	Sensitive and creatively productive
ANTOINETTE	Substantial and powerful, capable of substantiating substantial realities
APRIL	Capable of promoting individually characteristic emotions
ARABELLA	Full of energy, moves people
ARCHIBALD	Powerful, creative and very productive
ARIADNE	Of a powerful and sound nature in control of challenges
ARNOLD	Powerful and capable of spiritually enriching traditional substance
ARTHUR	Established, powerful and progressive
ASHLEY	Humanitarian and kind to all
AUBREY	Supports existing values for future benefit to others
AUDREY	Conserving best traditions
AURELIA	Accesses external energy to express creative energies
BARBARA	Filled with energy and giver of great and sound energies
BARRY	Producing immense power for good purposes
BASIL	Makes individual inspiration to community
BEATRICE	Bringer of energy-filled creativity
BELINDA	Creates emotional inspiration to others

BERNADETTE	Creator of very solid foundations
BERNARD	Generates and inspires solid change
BERTHA	Inspires creative development
BERTRAM	Evolves and nurtures power
BERYL	Focussing energy for future enjoyment
BETHANY	Initiator and builder of generative things
BETTY	Gives forth great substance for future benefit
BRENDA	Productive and capable of finding solutions
BRIAN	Productive and bringer of new ideas
BRIDGET	Develops sound constructions
BRUCE	Supports creativity
CALVIN	Promotes novelty
CAMERON	Nurturer of new ideas
CAMILLA	Nurturer and very emotional
CARMEL	Harnesses and nurtures energies
CAROL	Expressing lots of energies
CAROLINE	Employs exploring creativity
CAROLYN	Creative to benefit others in an exciting way
CECIL	Creative and outwardly sensitive
CEDRIC	Creates stable environments
CHARITY	Harnesses energy to bring charitable benefits
CHARLES	Inspired by external energies and including them in life
CHARLOTTE	Good energy with goodness spread to others
CHERYL	Lively and sharing openly with others
CHRISTINE	Full of creative energy subscribing to substance of life
CHRISTOPHER	Revealing new spiritual energy and projecting it
CINDY	Socially creative
CLARA	Logically clear and creative
CLARENCE	Capable of embracing new ideas
CLAIRE	Creative in an individual way to share
CLAUDE	Contributing to ancestral values
CLIFFORD	Creative, emotional, un-predictive but energetically sound

CLIVE	Gives birth to new learning
COLIN	Creating spiritual initiatives
CYNTHIA	Rich source of useful applications
CYRIL	Very energetic and emotionally expressive
DAISY	Obviously provides for the future
DANA	Caring for sensitive things to consolidate life
DANIEL	Capable of manifesting lots of emotional energy
DAPHNE	Source of lively energy
DARREN	Source of powerful energy, widely dispersed
DAVID	Supporter of firm traditions
DAWN	Full of promise
DEBORAH	Full of productive life
DEIRDRE	Sensitive to extreme human passions
DENNIS	Curious and exploratory
DEREK	Energetic draws in experience from past
DIANA	Solid and an explorer of mystery in everyday things
DOLORES	Shares emotions with others
DONALD	Gives inspiration to others
DOREEN	Interested in things of high value
DOROTHY	Very productive and protective
DOUGLAS	Investor and deliverer of good energies
DUNSTAN	Creating stability
DUNCAN	Creating lots of opportunities
DYLAN	Capable of giving to others in creative areas
EDGAR	Sound with access to energy
EDITH	Rule maker
EDWARD	Holder of potential resources
EDWIN	Explorer
ELIZABETH	Capable of bringing the spiritual into this world
ELLEN	Full of emotional expression
ELSIE	Spiritually expressive
EMILY	Nurturing and caring from this reality

EMMA	Sound nurturer
ERIC	Giving out productive energy
ERNEST	Gives birth to sound things
EUGENE	Well-born and adventurous
EVE	Bringing knowledge
EVA	Bringing life
EVELYN	Passes on knowledge and enthusiasm to others
FELICITY	Gathers in spiritual energy
FIONA	Thrives under unusual circumstances
FLORENCE	Inspires significant things
FRANCES	Senses intense external energies to share with others
FRANK	Curious and giving out life energies
FREDERICK	Producing benefits from core social values
GARETH	Competent, having great energy and serving life-giving sources
GEOFFREY	Good adventurer, bringer of good futures
GEORGE	Bringer of substance for all
GERALD	Focuses sound information into spiritual benefits
GERALDINE	Focuses sound information into spiritual benefits and distributes them
GERARD	Powerful person in established community
GILLIAN	Very spiritual person with adventurous spirit
GLADYS	Bringer of happiness
GLORIA	Bringer of good energies
GODFREY	Bringing and releasing energies for the future
GORDON	Contributes to well-structured progress
GRACE	Passing on creative energy
GRAHAM	Nurturing and conserving life energies
GUY	Handles important resources for the future with care
HANNAH	Full of life and adventurous, lively and full of emotion
HARRIET	Very energetic and contributing to society
HAROLD	Very lively bringer of quality substance to all
HAZEL	Accessing mysterious knowledge

HECTOR	Capable of encouraging energy
HELEN	Studies and cares for mysterious knowledge
HENRY	Exploring to produce vital futures
HERBERT	Very productive and energetic
HILARY	Enthusiastic and prominent processor of information to others
HILDA	Keen supporter of traditions
HOWARD	Bringer of surprising benefits
HUGH	Very lively
IAN	Questioner
IRENE	Investigative
IRIS	One with a balanced view
IVAN	Always curious
IVY	Conservative, caring and productive
JACK	Often moved to support others
JAMES	Nurtures those who are close
JANE	Explores may issues
JANET	Gathers together information
JANICE	Gathers lots of worthwhile things
JASON	Releases artistic novelties
JEAN	Considerate of others
JEANNE	Creative
JENNIFER	Very volatile
JENNY	Un-predictable but productive
JEREMY	Occasionally finely focussed on taking care of productive things
JILLIAN	A unique character filled with emotions
JOAN	Always prone to explore
JOANNA	One who successfully nurtures extremes
JOHN	Potentially very lively
JONATHAN	Innovative at producing new things of substance
JOY	Bringer of positive things to benefit many others
JOYCE	Works with others in a creative and positive way
JUDE	Capable of producing sound experiences

JUDITH	Producing core values
JUNE	Capable of facilitating useful research
KATHARINE	Outward looking with focussed energies
KEITH	Good at taking a sound position
KENNETH	Lively outward thinking, solid and questioning
KEVIN	Outward looking and open to unexpected results
LAURA	Inspired to express emotions and things energetically
LEONARD	Emotionally energy expressed in a firm way
LESLIE	Extremely passionately emotional
LEVI	Sensitive in processing information for others
LINDA	Sensitive to spiritual things in a practical way
LUCINDA	Creates new realities from spiritual inspiration
LUCY	Drawing on emotions to bring creative benefits
MALCOLM	Gathers and nurtures spirituality
MARCUS	Nurturing and spreading energy to others
MARGARET	Very sound and incredible energetic nurturer
MARTIN	Nurtures with attention to detail
MARY	Nurturing and preserving intense energy
MATTHEW	Nurturer of great substance with sometimes undefined reasons
MAY	Nurturing for future benefits
MICHAEL	Holding nurturing attitudes that enrich spirituality
MOSES	Life-giving
MURIEL	Takes care of spiritual energies
NEVILLE	Explores and releases latent energies
NICHOLAS	Self-conscious, creative and emotionally aware
NIGEL	Takes opportunity to improve many things
NOEL	Questioning and sensitive to spirituality
NOELLE	Questioning and forming rich spiritual environments
NORMAN	Well-focussed and caring for unknown things
OLIVE	Creates things
PAMELA	Outreaching, nurturing and spiritual
PATRICIA	Practical and creative, lots of energy

PATRICK	Explores this world cleverly
PAUL	Reaches out to understand simple spirituality
PAULA	Ambitious openly expresses emotion
PENELOPE	Cleverly reaches out to extremities
PERCY	Invests energy and creativity in the future
PETER	Intellectual builder of solid things
PHILIP	Inspire and adventurous individual
PHYLLIS	Extremely prodigious source of emotional energy
RALPH	Deals with outward expression in new areas
RANDOLPH	Explorer of mysterious energies in life
RAYMOND	Drawing on energies and conserving them
REBECCA	Sources and conserves important information
RICHARD	Gathers in and holds great energy and substance
ROBERT	Very lively and substantial
ROBIN	One who does unusual things
RODNEY	In touch with reality and investing in the future
ROGER	Very creatively energetic and fiery
ROLAND	Very creatively energetic and sensitive to surroundings
ROWLAND	Harnessing unusual energies of use
ROSALIND	Energetically gives out a lot in many areas
ROSE	Energetic and attractive
ROSEMARY	Energetic, attractive and nurturing energy to feed others
ROY	Conserves innocent energy
RUPERT	Brings together relevant things for good purpose
RUTH	Takes a clear and open path
SAMANTHA	Physical nurturer questions life
SAMUEL	Strong supporter of spirituality
SANDRA	Expresses herself in a humane way
SARAH	Enjoys life on Earth
SHEILA	Lively individual
SHIRLEY	Intimate source of spiritual enrichment
SIDNEY	Diligent student

SYLVIA	Passes on accumulated spirituality
SIMON	Cares for remote things
STANLEY	Naturally charitable
STEPHEN	Very ambitious
STUART	Aspires to bring about creative change
SUSAN	Develops physical exploration
SUSANNA	Physical and extremely adventurous
TERENCE	Substantial and focuses energy on controlling boundaries
THELMA	Nurtures human emotions
THOMAS	Conserving and giving forth enrichment
TIMOTHY	Drawing together good things for future benefit
TONY	Substantial, adventurous and enriching
TRACY	Very artistic
TREVOR	Intensely energetic in many directions
URSULA	Allows lots of emotions and other energies to flow
VALERIE	Energetic and alive, deep thinker and intellectual
VERONICA	Very good organiser
VICTOR	On the move and creating substance and new scenarios
VINCENT	Exploratory thinker and creative
VIVIAN	Very lively and very individual
WALLACE	Experimental and sensitive gatherer of creative information
WALTER	Adventurous emotional educator
WENDY	Finds ways of caring and saving things
WILFRED	Exploratory, takes risks to bring substance
WILLIAM	Unexpectedly emotional and caring
WINSTON	Exploratory but dependable
YVONNE	Reaching out with naive enthusiasm

First Names

I came to this topic because of an attitude of mind cultivated by the design of Modern Symbolic Labyrinths. These are arrangements of lines often with very strict spacings between them but capable of telling many stories depending on the angle at which you look at them. The description of the meaning or intuit in the letters is quite deep and forms the basis of the meaning of names. The analysis looks at the uppercase English alphabet. The lowercase was only introduced so one could write it down quicker. The alphabet is made up from straight lines and half curves assembled to form all the letters, angles and Arch Angles.

I believe that when a name is chosen, it is a magic time and highly valued time. Usually the person to whom the name is given and he or she who will be associated with it for a lifetime does not exist in any substantial form at the time of the naming.

It is not a simple logical operation. The parent does not say, "This is child number 2007."

The first question could be, "What are we going to call IT?"

Names may be chosen for both sexes, the final name used depending on the gender born.

The namers indulge in intuitive wishful thinking on a sub-conscious level plus part of the process seeks to ascribe conscious attributes. There may be a wish to get across some sort of valued continuity or an attempt to emulate another who went by that name. Surnames are more rigid and excluded from this book.

Whatever the motives, there is flexibility there and thus room for hidden meanings to creep in.

The ancients said that if you were lucky you grew into your name/s.

The list of names is not complete but it will be completed and you can participate.

The meanings are basic attempts but you may by studying the explanations of the meaning of the individual letters be able to refine your understanding of the names.

By comparing a name to the actual nature of the person carrying that name, you may be able to learn other details.

In this way, you can be empowered to choose names for your children and better understand the nature of those you know.

'In Search of the Holy Grail'

The Holy Grail has eluded man for many years but before we look into what and where it might be, let's look for something easier to find.

I am suggesting that our search is empowered by the knowledge I have assembled and written of in my Book of Names. This book which seeks to explain the hidden meaning of names draws upon my theories of the inner meaning or intuits in the individual letters of the alphabet in uppercase. There is an introduction to this in the Book of Names.

Key to the analysis is the focus on very simple visual lines, some straight and some in half curves.

All numerology is based on another simple concept, the creation of one, and then we move on to subsequent additions of various sorts.

The basic concept of lines can be applied in all sorts of ways to provide networks that are useful. The alphabet is one and the lines of longitude and latitude are others.

A helpful means of moving from one place to another is a track of some sort. An obscure track is a ley line but we have evolved other rigid configurations based on rails and we call them railways or railway tracks.

So in our search for the Holy Grail, let's put aside The Holy Grail and start with RAIL.

The letter *G* according to my analysis is a letter *C* joined to a letter *T*. The *C* means 'capable of creation' and the *T* is 'substance in this reality', so *G* means 'well done'.

The Freemasons have adopted it as a symbol of the Great Architect.

So the GRAIL is a RAIL that is well done.

If we look at our RAIL WAYS, we find a strong and resilient rail system that is available to all and accessible to many. Whilst a majority might have opinions that lead to the formation of various destinations, not all initiate the same destinations.

Someone else is responsible for installing the network.

Other sorts of routes are not visible at all as we fly along them in aeroplanes.

The RAILS may exist but human access to their reality is very varied. Most people on a railway sit and read, talk or glance out of the windows. Some sleep without knowing where they are. So long as they are basically safe, they do not care. At particular places some stopping might be invested in, so some can get on or off.

These are STATIONS. Their importance as points is determined by their relative position of the rail networks heading in opposite directions either side.

Another much simpler rail is what we use to help us open and close our curtains.

So we accept the concept of the railway and in one particular case, The London Underground, we tune into it in a linear way. The actual dimensions do not relate on any level to the reality below the surface but the rationalised rail network works for us.

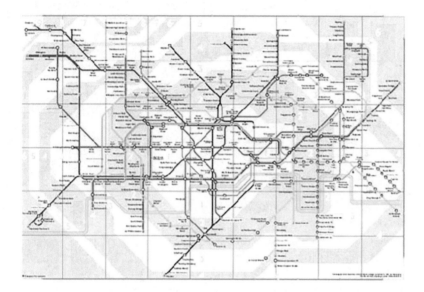

The railways have simple linear focuses often of an expansive nature. They reach out long distances. The lines may be straight but sometimes they curve. The established curvature is related to the positioning of intermediate points where perceived realities hold particular meaning. A sentence full of words and letters is the same. The meaning is contrived and where designed to meet a common purpose understood by sufficient users.

The letters in the alphabet have to be much smaller so they can be seen by the human eye. This, as Capability Brown said, requires something to be within twenty-seven degrees of the horizontal.

The word-system has become so useful that we have made the images as small as practical and placed them on pages so we can spin through quickly to gather in data.

The lines above and below words are hidden parallel rails within which we position the letters. In this whole scenario, it is important to approach things in the direction that will bring good benefit. A grail REVERSED IS A WELL-DONE LIAR.

So if you travel via various stations on a rail network, you only get a linear exposure to the surrounding landscape. With our alphabet, the meanings are supported by a linear configuration of letters but the letters and the words can be assembled to allude and bring experience of things outside the initial reality.

To use the network of rail travel, we have to CATCH A TRAIN. To understand much of what is in words, we have to CATCH SOMETHING IN THE NETWORK BUILT ON OUR UNDERSTANDING.

The whole of our earthly world is transacted by networks, be they ley lines, longitude and latitudes and a key way they differ is in their visibility.

To catch a fish, we contrive a very simple network. Key is that we know the size of what we want to catch and then we design a network that is smaller. CATCHING depends on being in the right place at the right time.

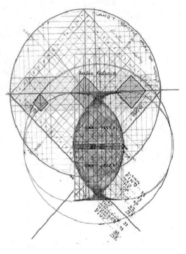

Another configuration of lines has been used to tune into The Holy Grail and that is the concept of a vessel. Vessels have always been very useful either as devices to store balms, drinks, grain and meat but the concept like a rail network of the lines of longitude and latitude can be applied on larger scale and key is we accept and use the inherent values to get to a valuable destination.

This has been linked to the pyramids and special numerology, so what is the journey and where does one get to if one sips along the way? Numbers were linked to the alphabet in the layout of the pyramids.

MAKE IMAGE BIGGER

Whatever network we use we do tend to go for the simple and not think too deeply. This may lead to the setting up of networks that bring fewer benefits and may bring about potential damage to the wider reality.

One of our underlying realities has been the atomic numbers locked into substances. Evolution in our time has led to the high numbers lessening, so an environment safe for fleshy beings arose and we evolved into it. The creation of new access pathways to these substances though application of scientific experiments brings potential dangers of radiation.

In the same way, playing around with RNA has released genetic networks that could be damaging.

One of the key items that we seek to CATCH in our networks is our REALITY and our LIFE.

Our letters and other substantial creations have contributed to symbologies that help us focus. Even the letters of the English alphabet are filled with symbolism.

I have used the word UNDERSTANDING and this is important. The definitive letter *A* has firm footings and its meaning is based on that understanding.

We are never very far from universally available symbols so 'getting our heads round' any topic involves our taking in all sorts of things.

Whether it be air in the form of breaths, food, drink, sounds and visible things, we get our head round them by enclosing them with a key part of our heads namely our skulls. They have twenty-two pieces and two heads are better than one, so the number forty-four has become an important measure in the Temple.

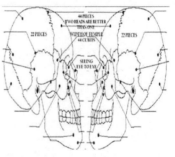

In appreciation of a symbol of something that is protected, strong and flexible and which will support someone for their useful life or reign, we adopt the spine with its on average thirty-three bits as a useful GUIDELINE.

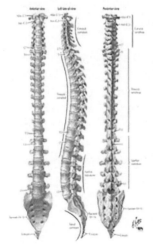

Horus reigned for thirty-three years as did Christ and the Freemasons use the numerology to construct the framework of an organisation with healing structure.

I am getting into complication.

Let us go back to the RAIL.
Its first letter is the letter *R*.

At the top of it is a circle, called the acupunct, as a symbol of some primal energies. It is symbolically a potential source of intense external energy. So a clear example is the sun.

It gives off an infinite number of energy lines as the Hadron Collider has done.

All we need to do is to show two of the lines and we create the letter *R*.

The letter *R* has evolved to serve us here on our perceived reality which we describe with our letter *A*. At the top of this letter is a spire. We may aspire but we tend to spend most of our life lower down, nearer to the foundations. That sense of our world but with access to the external energy was symbolised by the Egyptians in the form of RA.

It is in the beginning of **RA**IL.

We are the *I*s in life, so our relative position in the word **I** is NEXT IN LINE.

L refers to other energies, the more emotional and spiritual and possibly envisaged things. That's what should be at the end of a worthwhile rail. The letter *L* actually has a base-line that underlines. LEVEL is palindromic, so no slope whichever direction you are experiencing it in.

IF and *I* use that word advisedly. Our RAIL is badly made. It may include the **I**FFY letter and be FRAIL and our aspiration, albeit in a horizontal direction may lead to a **F**AILure.

Some very exact lineage is in place but it is not so simple as that. It is possible to build amazing structures based on this simple logic and much architecture and associated symbolism is invested with it.

However, the lines need not be so rigid.

I went into our local market and bought a knitted object. Here it is.

If we allocate a meaning to each coloured thread, we can see where they emerge along the woven line of existence that includes realities that are apparent and realities that are hidden. Let us apply part of what exists on a 'LEY' line between Cardiff Castle and The Temple of the Mount in Jerusalem.

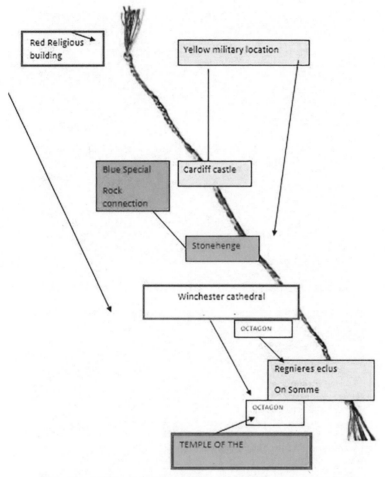

It is substantiated in the reality revealed by Google Earth.

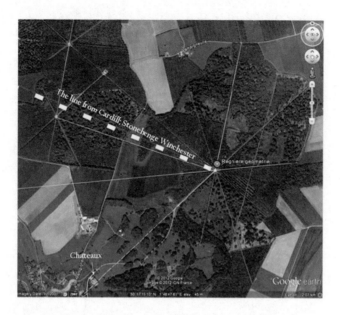

THE LINE FROM REGNIERES ECLUS IN THE SOMM LEADS TO THE TEMPLE OF THE ROCK IN JERUSALEM

So our railway tracks are very simply geometrical overlays that connect destinations or points of perceived importance in such a way that they are deemed useful.

The highly complicated realities that appear along the Cardiff-Jerusalem line are substantial and it is interesting that they are connected by a hidden rail. It is even more tantalising if we accept that their realities, whilst very different in appearance, have common threads and this is hinted at by the metaphor of the coloured, knitted band. If we accept that the word AND hints at more to come, the presence of a *B* in front adds to our understanding of more to come.

If our world is crammed with a tapestry of threads, then it should be possible through the application of expanding logic to design and create realities anywhere where one has access to the underlying network.

The network shown above is still very simple and linear.

Let's move away from the linear and use our alphabet as a tool.

In its normal mode of letters posed between upper and lower invisible parallel lines, we have something that many can read. It has become and established tool in our realities.

Let us move away from the chaotic configuration of its various pieces as below and form our alphabet.

ABCDEFGHIJK
LMNOPQRST
UVWXYZ

What if instead of applying a configuration that is a bit like a railway we assemble the lines by slightly changing the calligraphic shape of the letters and changing how they relate to each other spacially? We have created a net with the same basic components.

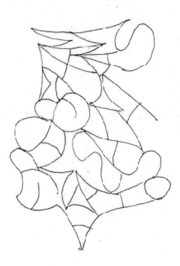

If we allow the concept of colour to enter, the basic letter concept begins to disappear but its presence is still controlling many things.

If we apply curliness to our basic network

And then other coloured dynamics, a new reality appears.

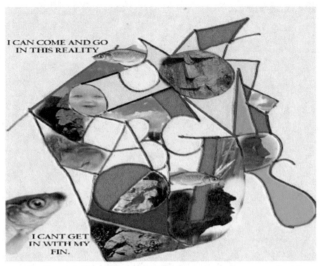

If we apply the curliness to the whole network, see what happens.

What if I say what you see below is a sort of Leyline map ?

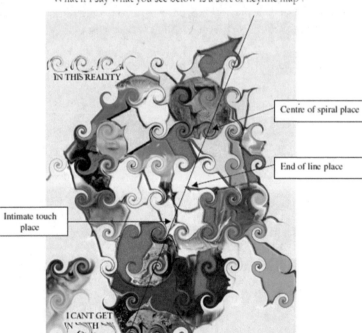

A line drawn may connect perceived interrelationships of the network lines that have as much to do with the network as the realities contained within it.

If we look at what we call a curtain rail, there is another clue. One has in place a straight line and around its extent we position a number of circles, curtain rings.

By applying human force, we move the attached curtains and if we are opening, the curtains reveal something hitherto hidden.

A lot of our cleverness has been applied with a device called a compass. By using it, we encompass all sorts of things. The way this is applied may be EVIL but best if we turn that round and invest in LIVE and bring about COMPASS ion.

What we reveal may leave us feeling AGOG and that may remind us of a recent network GOOGLE.

An ancient focus we have used to guide us in our BELIEF is based on Nature.

If we remove from the word the letter *I*, what happens?

I IS OUR INDIVIDUALTITY.

If we then add the letter *A* WHICH REPRESENTS OUR PERCEIVED REALITY, we have the word BE LEAF.

The leaf is a mechanism that draws in external energy from the RED sun *R* and it is green. We can identify more colours of green than any other colour. The green is due to the energies reflected from the chlorophyll within the leaves. So yes, the red of the sun can enhance the reading but reflection is also important. Originally the oxygen emitted was O18 and that was a number applied to ISIS the Egyptian symbol of total fertility. Exploring the leaves of this book may cause you to turn over a new leaf at any stage in the process.

HOLY?

H is the universal aspirant the breath of life.

O is birthing.

L the underlying spiritual energy.

Y means capable of taking in, holding energy for future beneficent use.

More Complicated Structures Emerge

Reality: .

We have to have something we can rely on to form a reality and whilst much of it can be exposed by logical thought, emotional response depends on much of it being hidden and inaccessible by normal thought processes. Whilst I am writing this in lowercase mostly, one should really take a step nearer to a fuller truth by reading in uppercase.

The word RELY then reveals the component *R* which refers to intense external energy and LEY which has within it spiritual and emotional energies capable of being absorbed, stored and given out (the shelving system of *E*) and *Y* which alludes to 'capable of taking in storing energy and information for future beneficent use'.

IN UPPERCASE, OUR ALPHABET IS MADE UP OF TWO SORTS OF LINES.
I SIMPLE STRAIGHT AND *C* HALF A CIRCLE

By arranging them such that the straight lines are either vertical, horizontal or at forty-five degrees and the half circles have the open side facing left, right or upwards, we can create the letters that link us to the intuits of meaning in our reality.

It is a very simple system but of course lines are defined things based on some investment between fixed points.

The simplest net can be made from overlapping straight lines and that can be useful. The lines of longitude and latitude are a good example as is a fishing net. If their usefulness depends on exactitude, then one will refine them to be accurate by trying to make sure that their points of origin are exactly measured distances apart.

But our reality is not as simple as that. A guitar or harp has some fixed points but what is between them has differing qualities. An application of external force changes their position and as a result something else emerges or is released, resonating sounds.

What if we take our alphabet through a number of stages as an entirety? We do not shuffle and sort the letters to give us words but we change other aspects of their apparent reality by adding colouring and then other aspects of reality.

Here Are The Bits

Bring three straights together and we have an *A*.

ABCDEFGHIJK
LMNOPQRST
UVWXYZ

Leonard Schlain said that all the cultures that write left to write like this have removed the goddess from their cultures.

Not surprising if that is the shape of the net; it only contains pretty rigid realities.

What if we configure the alphabet like a net?

What if we take another step and erode the straightness? Other cultures use more curly calligraphic 'letters'.

I am reminded of the day as young student at Kew Gardens when I saw a Birch Tree (Tree of Resurrection) with curls arising from its branches up into the sky. Then I saw the widest blade of grass on the mound of The Temple of Aeolus. A connection with earlier special geometries applied by Decimus Burton in 1844 when Decimus was forty-four years of age

Or we play around with LIGHT
Astrologers linked spots in the night sky to form things astronomy is based on.

One spot (a star) in The Plough might be four million light years further away than the next, but so what? It is The Plough because we believe it is.

Or we introduce light frequencies that bring us colours that are familiar (with what?)

Green plants, pink flesh, blue water and red energy

Here, the reality is enriched.
Faces real, faces in rocks

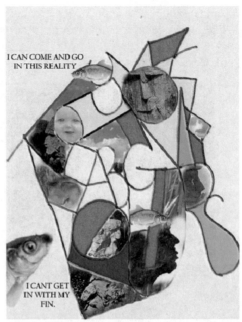

What we visualise within is containable. It is part of our reality.
If your network cannot retain it you lose it. The little fish can
swim in and out. The big one cannot get in.

The above is pretty straightforward.
What if I say what you see below is a sort of ley line map?

So a key thing is creating and installing lines as a basis for a belief system. We have lines of longitude and latitude but I do suspect that in spite of them being very simple de-lineation of space, the underlying network within which we survive is much more complex.

There are inherent forces that can destroy what we create and some simple proofs of this are there for all to see.

If one decides to create accurate shapes, then one often applies the concept of number to the concept of measure. This produces a distance and that distance may be between two points.

If we decide to create two words using the English Alphabet in uppercase, then we draw upon the two basic line configurations. One is the simple straight line and the other is the half curve. We may decide to tune into Egypt's Isis and Decimus Burton's special numbers applied to the main gates at Kew and the alignment of the Palm House we choose '18'. It can be a comfortable number when applied with inches as that is the height of most seats. We will ignore the measure and apply '18' of the seventy-five pieces of a full alphabet to form first of all the word LIVE. It has nine pieces all straight lines and eighteen ends. The *L* has four ends. The *I* has two. The *V* has four and the *E* has eight.

In its use, we ignore all this underlying structure but key is how we use it. If we write it backwards or read it backwards, then EVIL appears.

So is with the twin towers. A lot of evil is done without any awareness of what causes it and what leads to a mis-application.

Our alphabet is full of hidden realities upon which we build and sometimes these inherent meanings and UNDERSTANDINGS emerge on the surface. The letters affect the words and they do it with frequency and relative position.

If we apply this to what you have been doing as you read this, we can see some clues as to how the network for our reality is structured. The pentagonal geometry covering the Earth is simple compared with what really exists but we are positively pre-disposed to keep certain useful aspects of the network in our consciousness. In actual fact, we depend on much that is in our sub-conscious.

So we various configurations apply in many varying realities, so let's be creative with some other letters.

A E G P

RE-SHUFFLE

PAGE.
WILL YOU UNDERSTAND IF I SAY "GO TO NEXT PAGE?"

WHERE ARE **WE**?
HERE WE ARE.

The shape we call the *E* again appears and if we read it as we do when we first inspect a book, backwards usually, we see the word GAP appears.

PAGE
PAGEPAGEPAGE
EGAPEGAPEGAP
E_{GAP}E_{GAP}E

THIS THE LETTER E
IN ONE PLANE

What if we design a three-dimensional object that carries energy and information for transmission, a book?

The lines of the letter *E* reach out from the spine.

A leaflet is not what we are aiming for in the same way that one line of longitude or latitude has limited use.

The number of pages, including GAPS between, will be designed to accommodate the amount of perceived data to be carried. The load like our personal body is carried by the spine.

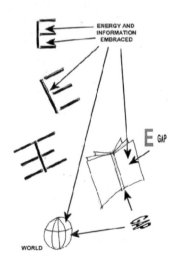

There are many networks and we tend to focus on those that have some form of logical simplicity. The lines of latitude and longitude are very simple but most plants use a creation of lines and their skeleton and substance between points based on a rather special harmony of numbers. I speak of Fibonacci sequences.

Key is the intuits at work. The letter *W* wherever it appears means 'we are not quite sure what is to follow'.

A focal point when something new is about to emerge is called a BEGINNING and here we see three letter *N*s. This is a testing letter, but calligraphically it is without some of the variation in direction that makes the letter *W*. Remove one of the lines that offers a change of direction in the *W* and you have a *N*.

Could this arch (mirrored) over the entrance to a church be a means of getting the mind out of this reality?

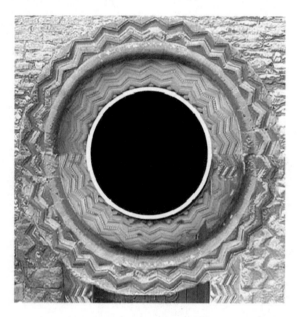

Here is an example of a *W* design as seen over old church entrances. Is this a way of getting the mind-set prepared to move into a new reality?

Recently, the World Wide Web has adopted the same imagery. Networks are in place and some of them are partially perceived and UNDER STOOD. However, one does not have to know everything about them so long as they are useful.

An example is the map of the London Underground. It bears little resemblance to the direction and levels of the underlying rails.

In this rendering a map shows you the best way to get to parties.

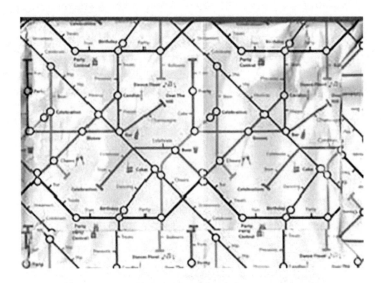

So you have your *E* spine in your body and the book has a spine that will support your on-going exploration. Your skull is protective and has great capacity.

The use of lines and colour was applied at Hampton Court Palace. The whole site is aligned with the summer solstice but cleverness was applied in the numerology of the railings around the palace. The railings are also green.

Gates and railings used to be flavoured with many colours but on the death of Albert Queen Victoria had most coloured black as a symbol of her loss of her beloved.

So leave the Appendix for now.

Henge History

A key time in the life of man in the temperate regions of the world was when he realised the potential benefits that could arise from applying what we now call agricultural skills.

The life of the hunter-gatherer where man roamed about changed dramatically. He had hunted for all sorts of animals, caught fish and other aquatic creatures, consumed all parts of plants, bark, leaves, fruits and roots. He collected wild honey and consumed the bodies of various insects.

Then the concept of cropping came into play. In Great Britain, enormous areas of land had been left with clay and this fertile substance made from the grinding of a wide range of rocks by the glaciers as they moved south, provided one sort of fertility.

Trees and scrub were removed and crops were sown and planted in these open areas.

The rich mixed flora grew all around and rivers still meandered in river valleys providing a continuing rich source of all the traditional hunter-gatherer foodstuffs to add to the new agricultural yields.

The key areas for cultivation were those above the flood level of rivers and on ground that was not to steep. Cultivation on steep slopes would lead to soil erosion and loss of crops. In more steep parts of the world terracing was employed but it was not necessary in most parts of Great Britain.

Man's accommodation changed from simple shelters often built under and around trees to small houses. They were made from locally available materials with a central erect upright vertical piece of a tree; angles of wood fixed in the ground and connected at the top. A gap may have been left to allow smoke from internal fires to escape. Woven materials ranging from flexible branches and twigs to straws of various types provided a weather-proof seal.

As the cereal crop agriculture expanded, the community developed communal solutions to the developing challenge of how to process massive crops.

The early cereal crops were from crops that released their grain quickly. We can see this sort of crop being harvested in Egypt. The seeds are gathered when ripe and any that drop are picked up.

Then the agriculture moved to cereals that held the grain tight, so wastage was reduced.

This then raised the need to effectively winnow crops i.e. separating the grain from the straw.

The straw was cut and gathered into stooks. Seven handfuls made a yealm. Each stook had seven yealms in it. They were then left for eight days for the grain to loosen and then it was taken to a communal thrashing floor. This was on a high spot so as to best tune into one of the engines of the winnowing, the wind. So from windrows it was taken to the henge. Hen means a high place, geat an enclosure. Our word 'gate' comes from Geat.

Initially, it would have been carried by hand but eventually carting developed.

One can imagine what happened when the various sharers of the harvest arrived with their share in the form of stooks. Entry would be controlled on an approach pathway or avenue and someone would assess the quantity being brought in by each shareholder. This would be measured in stooks.

TARF, ALGERIA

For a particular measure, the bringer would be given a token representing their share and that was called a dollie.

Made to a unique design for each site and with a hanger on the back so it could be kept safe subsequently, hanging back at home. The manager would keep all **the site dollies in a dolmen** on the bank that often surrounded the thrashing floors.

The contributor would then be given time to throw their stooks into a circle of stones called a threshold. In Greek this was called **Halos**. Then they thrashed the crop initially by stamping on it, throwing the stooks up into the air and letting the wind blow the chaff away.

The stamping gave rise to many dances such as Flamenco.

Later, the process was mechanised, initially by an ox pulling a slab with stones embedded in it and later by roller devices. The stones could be what we now find as shards and they could have originated form later dollies made form Dolerite stone.

When all the grain had been collected and taken away, the straw was stacked ready for the donors to collect in shares throughout the winter.

It was very bulky, so it would have been stupid to carry it any great distance. If the drainage needed improving, a groove was cut in the earth. Initially this might have been a simple spiral but at some time in the Neolithic someone came up with the design of the classic Type 1 maze.

It has a fascinating internal rotational symmetry and it caught on worldwide. This drainage groove was called a **riggoll**. Having formed the circle a next stage may have been the installation of a firm rock in the centre. This was to support the next part of the construction namely a tall upright pole. This central place later became **the tabernacle** and was sometimes called the shepherd's bower. There was sometimes access to it to allow inspection.

The term tabernacle is still used for the place where a ship's mast meets the hull and where lowering of the mast can take place so the ship can pass under bridges. The pole was tall and rigid and it was called a **rigpole**. This central part of the construction had to be held firm so at least four posts were fixed around the perimeter of the thrashing floor.

A ring was attached to the top of the rig, a **halo** and four **riggbands** stretched and were permanently fixed to the four permanent posts. These posts were called **riggbolls.** Another basic concept was that of the stake. A stakeholder hints at certain values.

Before the next stage, the stacking of the straw in a haystack, twigs were laid over the rigoll to improve drainage and aeration. The word 'twig' and its use in leading to a solution is still applied as we allude to understanding when we use the word. The rig pole may have been over seventy feet tall and in order to help prevent the haystack blowing over two things may have been done. Firstly instead of a circle, the **stack was shaped like an ellipse** so that it was a bit like a ship facing into the wind. Then a ring of smaller poles or riggbolls was put around and riggbands stretched from another halo down to them. The smaller riggbolls would have been put round the central rig in concentric circles but not in any accidental distance from the centre. Had there been one the design brief would have been for a storage unit that could be accessed

through the winter period and for there to be a good **measure of what was doled out**, so that **doling could continue throughout the whole of the winter period.** So contributors would be invited to come to get their shares at specific times. Their main role would be apportionment combined with a degree of support. There is another possibility and that is that as the haystack was built the riggbands would be attached and left in place perhaps with a marker attached linking to the donor and their dole. These times would be based on key **calendrical times** and these would be determined by **linking to various solar and planetary dynamics**. Archaeologists have discovered bones with inscriptions believed to help track lunar cycles.

Around 1500 BC, the Egyptians introduced the water clock (clepsydra), thus refining skills initiated tens of thousands of years before.

This is a later one in a temple in Turkey.

Part of the build might reinforce this timing awareness. Key riggbols or stones might indicate with their shadows what the dole measure should be at that time.

This system of calculation was applied later in Cleopatra's needles in Egypt.

Some might take their share of dole

away to where they kept the livestock needing food. There is evidence from Sweden of key representatives of the livestock gene pool being carried to the food store during the winter.

In some cases, they may not have taken straw away from the site but move it to **a field nearby where their stock was kept for the winter**. This more efficient way avoided the energy of moving livestock and moving large quantities of their food. This area may have been designed to better support doling out of stock in much the same way cattle are presented at markets now.

This is a site in Clatford in Hampshire.

To the south is a river.

Another design for stock would be a long **rectilinear enclosure**.

Decisions on whether contributors to the straw stock also brought livestock in may have been made in the autumn. An **autumn cull** of the inferior stock would have been made and those considered worthy of nurturing through the winter brought to the field or fields near to the henge. Times of feeding and also taking a way stock may have been tightly controlled so all received fair shares. **Periodic slaughtering** may have taken place and one wonders if the slaughter stone at Stonehenge is a clue to this.

The size and shape of the stone may relate to the animals slaughtered. It may simply be a focal point for those bringing stock to gather or to hand out the results of slaughtering.

Once the crop was safely stored there was some focus and celebration. It was given a name referring to the focus of benefits, firstly the HALO and the HALOS and then a special word to do with hope and optimism. WEEN.

The crop allowed the community to enter into WEANING, namely on-going life with some unknown outcome.

HALLOWEEN was a time of celebration and commitment rooted in man's connection with agriculture, the crop and his survival.

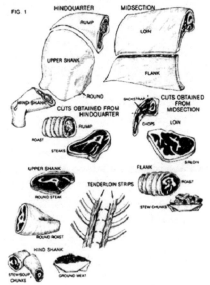

The slaughter may have taken place before the chosen dates for collecting straw and the resulting meaty food shared out.

The blood would have been saved and there is some evidence of enormous cauldrons. Offal may have been processed also so these more liquid benefits would have been doled out alongside cuts of meat.

A key part of the process would be hanging the carcasses safely for a while and **structures may have been in place to facilitate this.**

The bones would have been left or buried or taken to feed dogs.

Bones were also used to make tools and instruments.

As the winter progressed, the stack became smaller and **the riggbands were moved** and fixed to riggbolls closer to the tabernacle. This continued and when they saw **'the last straw'**, they looked around and saw the new grass was growing to feed their livestock they celebrated.

One thing they did was to grab the riggbands and dance around the rig pole. Our Maypole dancing includes a lot of people each holding a riggband so this residual symbolism could refer to the fact that donors would gather as a community and each would hold the riggband that represented what they had taken out during the winter.

There are quite recent records of a fence being put round the site because rats had filled the layers of twigs over the riggoll. In one Andover newspaper article one hundred and fifty years ago, it was reported that there were so many rats that the terriers put into to deal with them ran out of energy, so men had to go in with sticks and hit and kill the rats.

So in all this we have some clues to **groovy dances** including the dancing around the Maespal (Celtic for a field is maes).

In Sanskrit, 'Mas' means little points and that refers to the little points of new growth. 'Ne'er cast you clout till May is out' means: "Don't take your clothes off until all the new points are fully out in the form of leaves."

Another dance was the riggadoon (rig adorn).

The Morris dancer (name comes from Lake Moiris in Egypt) is the vertical male rig with riggbands or ribbons hanging from him and at times he may clash robust sticks together symbolising the killing of rats. The robust sticks were a form of priest.

The celebrations retained much of their symbolic value and are still performed today in the absence of that vital food chain. Whilst the key solar and lunar positions were used to create a measured calendar, it would not surprise me if the midsummer sunrise was used as a time of celebration but I suspect that could be the time when people signed in for the **oncoming commitment to planned harvesting, thrashing and storage**.

The corn dollie designers would be already designing the next year's credit cards and there might have been some reporting on the overall performance of the previous year. The word **feedback** comes into mind.

As the community became richer, the housing designed to support mankind became more sophisticated. The simple conical houses gave way to more rectilinear styles and because people were destined to live in them for longer periods, they became more substantial bricks made from mud initially and mixtures of chalk, straw, hazel branches and even cattle faeces led to more permanent structures.

From a time when the hals or thrashing floors were the only places where key gatherings took place, we moved to a situation where halls or special gathering places served other societal functions. With spare time to think and build power-structures, religions flourished and they needed special places for people to gather.

In the earliest times, they still celebrated key forces of Nature at large but as Man gathered power over Nature's forces some of these meanings were diluted.

One thing he did was to develop manifestations of grandeur so the small house he lived in for most people stayed the same size but special places like the halos of the haystack adopted special designs.

The haystack was large and stored straw, not people. The German for a maze is Dolhaus (house of the Dole or share), the Dutch Doolhoof. The French have a name for the maze based on the central wooden structure the Dedal. We in English tune into a much more basic meaning of Future Life as applied in Sanskrit by using the word 'maze'. The piece of ground where the initial Dolehaus was built was called a dolepiece.

The very first Grand Structures were simply buildings that were in the shape of the haystacks but with the central area or **tabernacle** not being a small space, just big enough for inspection of the place where the male rig met Mother Earth, but a large space big enough to contain a lot of people.

Some of the old symbolism in the haystacks and associated names was applied in ships. The rowers sat at the edge of the hull (not hall) on banks. (See meaning of U in appendix on letters.) Banks surround the halos. The sails were held up on a rig and rigging controlled the sails so that they tuned into the engine of the sailing and winnowing process, the wind.

Only recently have we used ships to move very large groups of people about as on cruises and we see in their design many halls.

In some old images, we can see a very old symbol of power at the bottom of the rig where it joins up at the hull, the ankh.

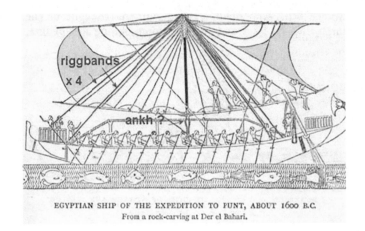

EGYPTIAN SHIP OF THE EXPEDITION TO PUNT, ABOUT 1600 B.C.
From a rock-carving at Der el Bahari.

The place where a mast can swivel so as to allow ships to pass under bridges is still called the tabernacle.

At the base of a rick pole, we see the same concept a tabernacle in the form of a stone.

We see also the various halo positions on the rig pole allowing the stooks to be protected as the size of the haystack was reduced through the winter.

So buildings became grander and even today they are built from natural plants, in this case reeds.

A possible celebration of Nature's powers and celebration of success in man's survival could be a design proposed by Bruce Bedlam. A roof over Stonehenge.

All the astronomical awareness and applied geometry to allow best tuning into Nature's calendar are celebrated in a design which basically tunes into a number of key aspects.

The shape of the haystack and also the shape of another device used by Nature to ensure ongoing life on earth, the beehive. All bringing CLEWS.

It is probably no accident that we say: TO BE OR NOT TO BE.

THE BEDLAM DESIGN

----------→

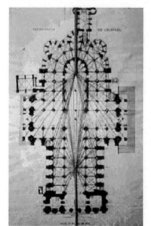

The Stonehenge site was well placed in a very fertile area and surrounded by many henges. Whilst all the others continued to provide opportunities for food storage the building at Stonehenge may have provided shelter for more governmental and celebratory activities. A society became larger and access by roads and shipping became more sophisticated the seats of power moved away from the springs of agriculture and that special structure was abandoned and as at Avebury bits and pieces were removed.

This building of grand places has occurred in all sorts of forms since but often-ancient symbolism remains as a foundation. The Cathedral at Chartres is on the site of an old henge and within it a maze celebrates in its numbers the **special number** relating to solar sunspot activity, eleven.

Sacred geometry has been applied and the centre of the maze is a key point where the fin joins the body of the fish and one connects with the body of the church. Vesica Pisces.

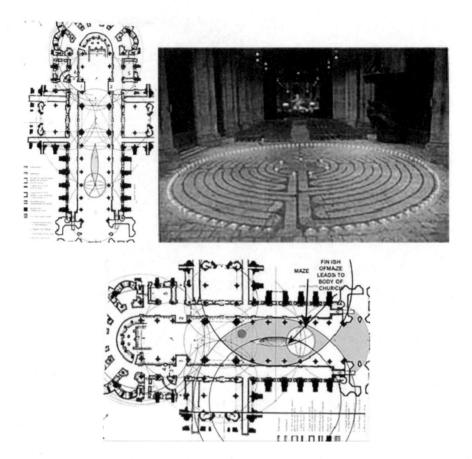

Agriculture underwent massive change when the early technologies based on wooden devices initially and then amalgams of wood and stone was influenced by the **discovery of metal.**

It probably arose accidentally from a fire that one day or night melted some special rocks to produce the first man-made metal. Man probably knew of gold already but gold does not have the strength to persevere under working pressures. The concept of being able to melt something allowed many to shape the metal by pouring into moulds or banging it into useful shapes

The resilience of metal and a total absence of planned obsolescence meant the man-made objects would have been kept for a long time and melted down when they ceased to perform effectively. No wonder there is little remains of the earliest tools.

As the metal agricultural devices came into use, the ability to sow in rows and weed rows increased production drastically. Harvesting with metal sickles and scythes allowed cleverer design of straw-length procedures. Initially, all activities were done by fit humans but later heavier loads of work were achieved employing cattle and eventually machinery similar to what we use today.

The early bringing of locally grown produce to the stacks by hand was replaced by carting and wherever feasible by access to ships on nearby rivers. Tracks or ways over high ground would have been made secure by creating causeways but most riverside areas would have been very boggy due to the meandering nature of rivers then empowered by much more postglacial flows.

The only people who spent a lot of time at the henge sites were the managers. Some of them may have chosen to be buried there or some may have died at times when it was so busy they simply had to be buried sooner rather than later on site. The initial sites were exposed to the weather so only attended when work needed to be done.

Key in all of this is simple functionality and then engrandisment as the community became richer and had more time and resources to devote to additional entertainments.

Some of the sites provided opportunity for spiritual linking not just with the earth but with the planets, the solar system and other dimensions. Key to this linking however was keeping an eye on what time of the year it was. Keeping an eye?

Management was the key and a Roman team was called the Flamen Priests. A priest is a practical device that is used to make the transition from life to death as fruitful as possible. Fish priests are the objects still used by fishermen to kill the fish effectively, so the remains can be used effectively and the passing is quick. They are small but larger ones are applied to kill rabbits. The Flammen priest wears a special cap or hood and this is made of lambskin as was and is still used at the top of haystacks to protect the straw, protruding from the top of the priest hood an olive post, echoing the rig at the top of the haystack. He carries something that alludes to the word AND (more to come) and it is a WAND. In addition to their practical roles, there is a clue that he can bring about spiritual enrichment in a world to come.

By the time we reached ancient Rome, the race of priests called The Flamens may not have danced at all. There is no record of this, but that does not mean this was not part of their role. There was a list of responsibilities:
The twelve **flamines minores** could be plebeians. Some of the deities whose cult they tended were rather obscure, and only ten are known by name:

- **Flamen Carmentalis**, the flamen for Carmentis
- **Flamen Cerialis**, for Ceres
- **Flamen Falacer**, for Falacer
- **Flamen Floralis**, for Flora
- **Flamen Furrinalis**, for Furrina
- **Flamen Palatualis**, for Palatua
- **Flamen Pomonalis**, for Pomona
- **Flamen Portunalis**, for Portunes

111

- **Flamen Volcanalis**, for Vulcan
- **Flamen Volturnalis**, for Volturnus

Much of our vernacular history is not being substantially recorded. They wore a sheepskin hood with an olive stick sticking out of the top and a sheepskin cover was on top of the giant haystacks to help keep the rain out. Today in Ladakh, the same technique of haystack building is still used.

They were maypole lookalikes. The Flamen also carried a symbolic stick and it could be that it was a sort of priest. Even now a priest is a solid stick used to kill fish or a slightly larger, heavier one used to kill rabbits. So the transition between a living being and a sacrifice to produce food and on-going life was adopted in a sort of religious way. Priesthood?

On a more basic level, the word AND hints at more to come and the letter *W* before it which means "whatever follows this symbol, we are not quite sure about" alludes to the power of a WAND. So the Flamen's stick is not heavy as it is applied symbolically to spiritual dynamics.

Flamenco dancing has two main components. One is the agricultural cereal stamping and the other where the male uplifts his arms alludes to the cattle and their horns. The cattle were what was fed with the straw though the winter. There is mention of cattle in Sweden being carried to the stack at the end of the winter, so weak they were. The prime aim was to get the best genetic material through to the next spring. An end of summer cull reduced the load as inferior stock was killed and eaten.

Sukot is The Feast of Ingathering and it happened in the autumn when the crops were harvested and safely stacked. At the foot of the rigs on old ships, where the male rig touched upon the female hull, there was a very hard piece of wood called a tabernacle. It still exists on modern boats that have to drop their mast to go under a bridge. I believe the base of the haystack was also called a tabernacle and another word for tabernacle is OHEL.

The letter *U* is transitional so Hal becomes Hull. How linked all this is this to the call to the dance OHAL. In another language, the word TABERN alluded to a cellar, a place of storage.

This place in the centre of the haystack where the male symbol entered the female Tellus mater, the Earth mother, was so special as a key place of union at the very core of the stack of food that would help the populace through the winter.

An old Hampshire farmer told me of old haystacks where a small place was kept clear in the centre. It was probably for basic maintenance and accrued special value from that. Was this the origin of another name associated with mazes, Shepherd's Bower?

The Morris dancer has his riggbands hanging and he also carries a stick. Is that a priest for killing the rats as reported in a Hampshire newspaper one hundred and fifty years ago that multiplied in the twiggy substrate over the rigoll and under the haystack?

The Romans developed a series of Gods and they were basically focused on job descriptions:

- **Vervactor**, "He who ploughs."
- **Reparator**, "He who prepares the Earth."
- **Imporcitor**, "He who ploughs with a wide furrow."
- **Insitor**, "He who plants seeds."
- **Obarator**, "He who traces the first plowing."
- **Occator**, "He who harrows."
- **Serritor**, "He who digs."
- **Subruncinator**, "He who weeds."
- **Messor**, "He who reaps."
- **Conuector** (Convector), "He who carries the grain."
- **Conditor**, "He who stores the grain."
- **Promitor**, "He who distributes the grain."

More or less, the same tasks are used today.

Much of the world is under various sorts of threat due mismanagement of the banking (Bankh?) system. Man's survival carries with it basic dynamics which are inherent and essential for survival.

In the case of nutrients, our bodily functions have required the same ingredients for millions of years, although the menus we select from have become more varied and complicated when viewed from the exterior.

So it is with many aspects of our life and key to best management is a proper understanding of what it is all about. This paper is about trying to get back to basics. We need to look at some of the words we are using to see if they have within them clues to the best solutions.

Understanding is one key word. Without a sound foundation beneath anything, little can stand firm. That understanding is vital. The best solution alludes to BES the Egyptian god that represented Goodness. They said in ancient Egypt that if a child smiled in its sleep it was because it had seen Bes in a dream. Yes, a God, whatever that means, but more importantly a word that refers to a basic force worth investing in and celebrating.

The topic here is core to understanding man's survival and the dynamic of banking.

Bes was a bringer of goodness but that concept is universal. See here an image of Bes and another Mexican statuette also bringing something to feed one.

As Marc Chagall did with his Minotaur in Chichester Cathedral (see Appendix) the key present is seeds of ideas.

THE ORIGIN OF MAZES, LABYRINTHS AND MORRIS DANCING

It is easy to make mistakes in interpreting the past and one of the biggest errors extant is the naming of mazes as labyrinths. If one studies the ancient words and their associations, it is clear that some adjustment has to be made to some current theories.

I am always amused by the spoof supposedly done in 4000 AD of the old programme Animal Vegetable and Mineral. In that first programme in the 1960s on English TV, an item would go round on the turntable and perhaps Sir Mortimer Wheeler the eminent archaeologist would get it first.

"Yes, I think you will find this is from the Merinde period in Egypt, 4800-4300 BC and a votive pot associated with burials in a fetal position. I think you will find it was discovered at 9:11 am on the 7th July 1881..." etc. etc.

In the 4000 AD programme 2000 years plus later, the object on the turntable is what we know to be a teapot.

*The first archaeologist holds the teapot and says, "These were very common around the 20th Century. The remains have been found throughout the continent but mainly in Great Britain, which at the time **we think** was separated from the rest of Europe by a large river which some think was called the River Carnal,"* We know it was/is The Channel.

"The general theory is that it is some sort of musical instrument."

The item is handed to the next 'expert'.

*"I agree with Professor Weinhardt. I have just completed an eight-year study financed by Oxford University and **although the music has never been found**, it is thought that the instrument was placed to the lips (he puts the spout in his mouth) and blown.*

This valve (he lifts the lid) then enabled the musician to play appropriate music.

The range of variation in the music must have been very great as the designs of these instruments are so varied. The rounded shape hints at some sort of Birthing Goddess being celebrated. The presence of remains of the plant <u>Camellia or Thea sinensis</u>, (Latin names of Tea Plant) whose fallen red flowers in Japanese mythology allude to the Samurai, hint at the unity of male and female."

The item is then handed to the next 'expert'.

"What I am going to tell you next has not been revealed yet.

The musical instrument theory is further supported by the theory that the performances sometimes involved hundreds of players, thus necessitating the wearing of some ear-protection. We have found thousands of fragments during a recent excavation at a place archaeologists deem a location for healing ceremonies.

Last week, a sign was discovered by an entrance avenue similar to the one at Stone Hinge and it clearly said London Re-cycling Centre. The involvement of many players playing very loudly is further reinforced by our finding amongst the remains of these instruments what we think are protective earmuffs. This throws some light on the enormous scale of these ceremonies possibly associated with the massive giving of the wide range of gifts also being found at these places and a belief in recycling of the soul into a new world.

Sometimes very well decorated earmuffs have been found.

These were worn in pairs with a thong joining a handle on each muff. The thongs have not survived."

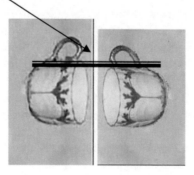

I call this **teapot** and it is present in much of the so-called knowledge about our past.

William Matthew Flinders Petrie was very critical of some of the ways knowledge was being accessed and used and this neglect is still in place. "Nothing seems to be done with any uniform or regular plan. Work is begun and left unfinished; no regard is paid to future requirements of exploration, and no civilised or labour saving devices are used. It is sickening to see the rate at which everything is being destroyed and the little regard paid to preservation."

He was speaking of physical work but the loss of ancient mental understanding is the cause.

Egypt had a highly developed economy based on agriculture. People who did agriculture lived necessarily in the country. Lake Moeris was part of the water economy that served the agriculture and a great city was built there supposedly by Min. The words MOOR and MORE refer to plenitude. The annual flooding of The Nile was tuned into by efficient drainage systems and agriculture.

Min was the ithyphallic god of the Egyptians but my view is that **many of these so-called god and goddesses' names and personalities were only ways of human beings exploring their own psyche without the limitations of the self and logic. Spiritual experiences were recognised and honoured as a part of everyday life.**

We still refer to particular people as stars. They can be actors, sportspeople but the inherent description alludes to "higher than the rest of us, brighter than the rest of us, distant, difficult to reach", forces one might aspire to invest in.

Initially no one 'worshipped' as we call it, they all **celebrated** the dynamic essences of life and needed to get their heads round key dynamics. Many of the early names of Gods and Goddesses were simply ways of focusing on fairly complex spiritually related forces. The Roman for 'country folk' is pagi and the beliefs and celebrations, not worships, of these folk were later lumped into the word 'pagan beliefs'.

The corporate religions later based themselves on the early beliefs and as time passed, the individual's own personal access to his or her spirituality was channelled by highly structured, organised and controlled priesthoods. If one subscribes to the 'later developed-religions concept', every artefact found on ancient sites may move from being 'an accidentally abandoned object' or a 'deliberately discarded object' or a 'lost object' or 'something hidden for future use' to become a sacred object. Certain objects that are designed to be unique for a purpose may have an associated design on them. It might be simply for decoration with no religious intent. A female symbol thus analysed may turn the object into a votive goddess object when there is no real evidence for this. It is simply art being used to celebrate an aspect that is considered favourable.

The lives of all folk were and are still tied closely to Nature. The range of crops grown and gathered from the wild even before the very early Neolithic was massive.

Archaeological digs at Ohalo near the Sea of Galilee have found eight hundred species, the remains of which have been found in stones used by early chefs for grinding. What does OHALO refer to?

Then they grew crops in a more mixed way and harvested them. Certain techniques became universal not least because of their practicality. Selected crops capable of producing nutritive seed in one growing-season at worst, sometimes two crops, were sown widely in areas cleared of forest. Nature was tuned into and the sowing of Winter Wheat, then and now is best done on

October 31st. The end result would be an enrichment of the yield in the halos or thrashing floor and doing it properly was weening. So Halloween.

A wider range of sowing was done around February 14th and the value (VAL) was achieved by using (TINES) properly, so VAL-en-TINE. The birds were tuning into the same period by mating. The later festival when the eggs hatched was Oestre, so Easter.

Nuts were amongst the crops that could be harvested and stored easily and safely to get the population through hard periods. A key nut is the almond. Its ovarian-shaped seed was much respected and later symbolic naming was based upon it.

The almond is <u>Prunus amgydalus</u> and a city Magdala was celebrated, as was the name of a special woman the Magdalene. Some weeding took place and at the end of the growing season a harvest took place. Initially the cereals ripened and dropped their seeds, so harvesters had to move in early on and cut the clusters of seeds from the top of the stems. One has to **lean over to glean**. Later cultivars (a cultivar is a special plant selection adopted by man) were used which held the grains tight. The reapers cut the crop, not **a cut above the new norm**, but close to the ground. Then they gathered the crop by hand into bundles. A special name was given to each of the seven grasps (YEALMS). It was only when mechanised sowing in rows came into play that farming took a massive productive leap and the labour input per acre reduced. Seven yealms made **a stook**. Thatchers used the same term and some still do, but a thatcher's stook was made of five yealms.

These stooks as we later called them were left in rows, some say for Nine Days or Nine dews, so as to loosen the grain. The aim was perhaps two fold, first to dry the straw and to get better access to the rich grains. Another reason may have been to facilitate the counting of stooks and subsequent organization of the next stage. The two engines of the drying process were the sun and the wind. That's why they were put in *windrows*. Then the stooks were carried to a higher place. They may have been carted there and the haul roads may have been consolidated or show signs of wear. At Marden henge, we see how the entrance to the area within the bank is consolidated with imported gravel, a causeway. Hen is one word for a high place. Hengeat combines hen for a high place with geat, an enclosure, from which we get the word gate. At this place, the threshing took place. A circular row of stones prevented the grain from spreading sideways as the grain was thrashed. This was done originally by stamping upon it.

The stones held the threshings in place and this was called **the threshold** and only the chosen ones could tread there to do this special work and derive the vital provender. Even now, not just anyone can cross a threshold.

Stamping went on all day. This stamping became part of the ancient dances.

The high place was windy and therefore not the warmest place to live so the high value, low-volume grains were taken down to more sheltered dwellings and the bulk of straw, which was much taller than modern strains,

117

was stacked. Why waste effort moving it again? Some grain was placed in underground pits, again to save transport.

In this Egyptian relief (1300 BC), we see crops almost six feet high being cut by hand.

In order to ensure that the enormous stack did not fall over, it was sometimes built in the round or elliptical with a stout central rig or rick pole. It may have been a large tree and examples have been found in 2008 of inverted trees stuck in the earth. It might have been over seventy feet tall. In Frazer's Golden Bough, we read of a giant tree being cut each year and pulled by many oxen out of the forest. This was called a dedal. The French word for maze is 'le dedale'. It is interesting that this rig pole in a ship is called the 'mast'. The word is MAS plus the letter T that alludes to 'substance in this reality'. Tell me to a T, we say.

The up-turned trees may have been used with the roots facing upwards, thus providing a place to which the riggbands could be fastened. Later, this became the halo-shaped ring at the top of the rig in a position closest to the life-giving sun. Rig top haloes were adjustable.

We can see various aspects of the meaningful symbolisms in Indian mythology.

In addition to the straw, other vegetable matter such as twigs was included particularly in the more temperate regions. The higher ground afforded drainage but to render this more effective a drainage trench was dug. One of its names a riggoll (circular ditch in the ground) gave rise to the rigolletto and many groovy dances. At some stage, possibly in the Neolithic, some human brain invented what we call the classic maze, the uni-cursal one-way route from centre to exterior. This fashion spread worldwide.

It worked practically but it also fascinated man as the lines within it were subject to constant change. **Change has always been one of the key mysteries** of life and something we must learn to deal with. The only other natural expression of a similar internal rotational symmetry of the maze, albeit simple, is found in the courting dance of the tortoise.

The ropes that held the hay tight were called riggbands from which we get the word ribbons. They were held in place by concentric riggbols or rigg boles set in the ground and a good example of these bolls can be seen at Woodhenge in England.

Four bols were permanently attached to the rig so as to keep it upright and this could be the reason behind the design of the Saffron Walden Turf Maze. See Egyptian punts later.

As time progressed, the observant might have noticed that key alignments of the sun would give them clues as to how far through the winter they were, clues that would allow them to more effectively use their store of food.

The early wooden constructions would have been very numerous and their size related to their volume of straw and richness of cropping in the area. A henge the size of Stonehenge seventy-four feet high would get five hundred cattle through the winter.

In the more sophisticated locations, those approaching with their stooks first of all underwent an inspection and valuation of their stock in hand. At a key point on the approach avenue, a haul-road a sort of sentry post. This might have been substantiated in the form of a stone, a heoul stone. Some had more stock than others and those with the most were well-heouled.

As the community brought in their straw, they were given tokens that they could exchange for their dole or share throughout the winter. These corn dollies were varied in form and of course each year they had to be discernibly different in design. There would have been geographical difference also in the same way we have various international currencies. They do not remain in the archaeological record for two reasons. The first they were invalid twice round and they rotted quickly. A temporary store might have been needed to provide shelter and security for a whole lot of corn dollies before they were disseminated to visiting dole bringers, could this have been the origin of dolmens?

Control of stock allocation could have been achieved by referring to solar, lunar and other planetary positions and oscillations like Venus. Hence many henges show special alignments.

One has only to read Prehistoric Phases by Hodder M Westropp published by Bell and Daldy, Covent Garden 1872 to realise that major misunderstandings of their function has become established.

These dolmens existed/exist in their thousands and if we look carefully, we can see that they were probably used for storage. Access was controlled and the nearest I have seen to our wall cash-machine is a dolmen in India.

RUSSIAN

Dollies were taken home and hung up out of reach of things that might eat them; part of the design of Corn Dollies is a hanger at the back. Dolmens are often situated in the banks around the henges, so maybe this is the original banking system.

Look carefully at the dolmen near to one of the henges in this old image. What's inside? The time when the dol was signified was very special and could be called a rite. The word 'write' reveals what a rite is. The 'w' means 'whatever follows this symbol we are not quite sure of' but what follows assures us that there will be something of value, namely a word, many words and a useful sentence. The letter 'D' alludes to 'hereditary substance', so the word DID and DAD echo that. It is perhaps no coincidence that DOLERITE is connected with a very special place of doling out, Stonehenge. Stone Dolerite Dollies might have replaced Corn Dollies.

The corn dollies will have been destroyed once the hand-over of straw took place and stone dols may have been smashed leaving the remains we call shards. If you analyse the words SHARED and SHARD, there may be a clue. The *E* has gone from the word

SHARD. Look in the appendix 'meaning of the letters' and the letter *E* means 'capable of taking in, holding and giving out energy and information'. Shards do not allow this and if you smash it, once you have SHARED, you cannot re-use the bits to get shares of the crop. Of course nothing was wasted and some of the shards could have been put in the bases of the wooden slabs used for thrashing. Dolmen lookalikes may have been shelters for henge Managers.

Recent excavations at Marden henge have exposed the foundations of a building on the bank. It is somewhat larger than some of the typical dolmens shown above but we also have an interesting addition which some say might be an indication of it being a sweat lodge, namely remains of fire-scorched earth outside. These devices depend on stones being heated outside an enclosure and then brought inside to warm a space.

Rather than what has been found at Marden being a sweat lodge, I would pose that it may have been a safe way of heating the dolmen store of very flammable corn dollies. It might also have made the place more habitable for the dolmen guard who had to stay there for the period of dole giving.

Another interesting feature is an extended area of reinforced ground by the entrance to the Marden dolmen and this would have been very practical to accommodate the extra footfall at the approach to this larger than average dolmen.

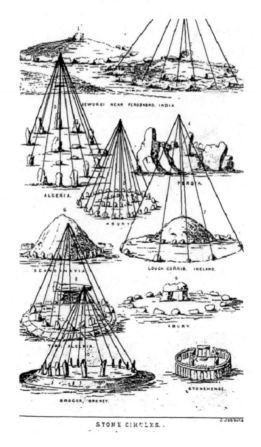

STONE CIRCLES.

This concept of the dole or share came down through the ages into more recent languages. The place where the stack was built was known as the dolepiece or the winding piece. The various components of the design of this immense store were used to describe it. We might say Tesco, Waitrose or Sainsbury's (British retailers) but we mean shop. Our Maze refers to the promise of things to come; the German name for a maze, Dolhaus and the Dutch Doolhoof refer to the Share House and the French for a maze is Le dedale going back to an even earlier form of vegetation celebration focusing on the dedale, the largest tree anyone knew.

The dedale gave rise to the Egyptian Djed a sacred column that symbolised the rigid core of the bole of the tree and this became the centre of the haystack. The central pole took over and in the typical symbology reminded folk of the rigid and sometimes inflexible attributes of the male and his phallus, also of the attributes of permanence and slow steady change associated with the tree. The name 'Daedalus', like all names, had value through association with these positive things. The fact that the Daedalus of the Minoan legends was an impostor is nothing new. Everything he did failed and in the end the gods took his only son, Icarus, in punishment.

If clients had only read his name backwards the might have avoided trouble. Example LIVE in reverse is not good, EVIL.

Our use of the word 'Maypole' however hints at the real holistic understanding that these people had, for the maze was carved out in mother earth so the two, like the Pharaoh'ankh, represented unity. Maespal.

There is a twenty-seventh letter of the alphabet now no longer in use. The ampersand looked a bit like a Z but was pronounced Y. The Celtic for a field alludes to this place of future beneficence, namely a maes.

We must look deeper though, for the word 'mas' is from Sanskrit meaning 'little points'. Which little points? Well, the most important little points on Earth, the ones of new-growth. They are hinted at in the mosaic shown elsewhere in the appendix. They knew that without the power of photosynthesis, as we call it, and the green, the energy from the sun could not be fixed and the plants could not produce the carbohydrate or oxygen. If we look even deeper, we see these letters alluding to a form of nurturing that would bring benefits in the future. The word MAY is a clue to this. Min was no good on his own; there had to be Isis and a whole panoply of representative forces under different names. Delving more deeply we can look at the meaning of Y. I believe the intuit, as I call it, in this letter is 'capable of taking in and holding energy for future beneficent use'. A tree is a real example and the letter Y is like a tree in simplistic form.

In later sophistications, numbers came into play and the number of Isis was eighteen. How weird that modern science sees Oxygen18, not the O2 we now breathe, as a first substance creatively serving our evolution!

All the odd numbers were male and the evens female. So birth could not be until the two nines are brought together. Eighteen is female.

So the threshing floor came to be known as HALOS.

S wherever it occurs alludes to 'being of the flesh'. 'To be' in various languages IS, IST, ESSTE, EST, so HALOS is a special place for us in our corporeal state. Above and out of reach a HALO, no *S* present and a ring held the riggbands high above the ground closer to the heavens. The halo encompasses what we can reach within our life awareness, so it sits around the spire.

Each riggband is shared power in protecting our reality, the harvest, and any religion can be like a collection of different riggbands serving common purpose. The dolhaus only works if all work together.

Later, the call to the dance was OHAL OHAL and where do we gather now to dance but in the dance HALLS. Many other gatherings considered important happen in HALLS. I mentioned earlier a place called Ohalos. 'Hael' is a word associated with the current term 'Wassailing', again the heaol associating with the beneficial provender from halos and other yielders of goodness, like trees.

The OMPHALOS was another key symbol. It was called the navel of the world. It was placed in key geographical places as a stone carved with a network. The network alluded to umbilical cords but also key transitions of Venus in its numerology. The OM alluded to OMEGA, some substantial finality. *O* is birthing and *M* is nurturing. A reaching out *P* followed by a Thrashing floor HALOS. Not the male PHALlus.

There must have been all sorts of dances starting with the stamping dances. Flamenco is classic thrashing dance. The high spots used in Spain were often ridges. Ridge, Rid, Rig. All these names allude to the powers at work in these places and the benefit to be derived. The dancing sometimes took on special choreographies associated with the rigolls and the word Troy alludes to the turning. IF YOU DRESSED UP LIKE A BIRD, YOU TUNED INTO THE FACT THAT BIRDS WERE ALWAYS ASSOCIATED WITH ORACULAR MESSAGES. A LITTLE BIRDIE TOLD ME. Why is there a bird on top of the steeple? To tell us which way the wind is blowing. The cranes were ancient signs of a change in the seasons as they migrated in their millions. Geranos was the crane dance. Geranium is the cranesbill flower. Flam is in another dancing reference, namely the Flamingos.

Everyone danced and of course some were better at it than others. That is the same now and anyone who has done flamenco will know that you have to be extremely fit for a start. Its origins were not dashing about from side to side but a steady pounding in a restricted area. I suspect it was a male job initially.

The thrasher would have to keep his *feet on the ground* when at work but when the time came to celebrate he might let loose and enter a sort of trance. I have experienced this personally at a Divali festival in Guyana and this step into the shamanistic is admired for different reasons, especially if the dance is inspired and entertaining. I suspect some of the celebratory dances around lake Moiris in Egypt, a place associated with the first labyrinth, were like this and as society became specialised the dancers took on almost full-time shamanistic roles. By the time we reached ancient Rome, the race of priests called The

Flamens may not have danced at all. There is no record of this, but that does not mean this was not part of their role.

They all had detailed job descriptions associated with agriculture. They wore a sheepskin bonnet with an olive stick sticking out of the top and this sheepskin cover was on top of some of the giant haystacks to help keep the rain out. At the base is a blob of wool. Today in Ladakh, the same technique of haystack building is still used.

They were maypole lookalikes.

Flamenco has two main components, one is the agricultural cereal stamping and the other where the male uplifts his arms alludes to the cattle and their horns. The cattle were what were fed with the straw through the winter. There is mention of cattle in Sweden being carried to the stack to be fed at the end of the winter, so weak they were. The prime aim was to get the best genetic material through to the next spring. An end-of-summer cull reduced the load as inferior stock was killed and eaten.

Sukot is The Feast of Ingathering and it happened in the autumn when the crops were harvested and safely stacked. At the foot of the rigs on old ships, where the male rig touched upon the female hull, there was a very hard piece of wood called a tabernacle. It still exists on modern boats that have to drop their mast to go under a bridge. I believe the base of the haystack was similarly called a tabernacle and another word for tabernacle is OHEL. Old pictures show natural stone reinforcement and also a more sophisticated tabernacle, possibly octagonal.

The letter *U* is transitional so Hal becomes Hull. How linked all this is this to the call to the dance OHAL. In another language, the word TABERN alluded to a cellar, a place of storage.

At Ohalo two, an ancient, now submerged, site near the Sea of Galilee where over twenty-three thousand years ago man carried out early agriculture, evidence of one hundred taxa (types of plants) have been found.

If we look closely, we can see another key Egyptian symbol at the foot of the mast, the ankh. As man's life became better filled that word was associated with a key letter to do with plentitude, the letter *B*. The Bankh emerged as a place where valued things of substance were cared for. Bring and Build all have *B*s and that's quite safe. Baby is OK. One has to be careful if too many appears as in BUBBLE as whilst they can be great in the right context, they do tend to burst, so not a thing to be invested in for stable, long-term benefits.

See how similar this Egyptian ship (1500 BC) is to the haystack.

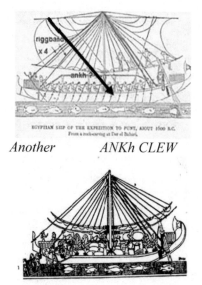

Another   *ANKh CLEW*

The place where the rowers sat 'banks'

    This place in the centre of the haystack where the male symbol entered the female Tellus mater, the Earth, was so special as a key place of symbolic union at the very core of the stack of food that would help the populace through the winter.

    Many henges are built close to existing rivers which in post-glacial times must have been wider and deeper. Stonehenge is an example. Ships looking like floating haystacks could have been used to move valuable grain from the larger sites such as Marden Henge. At that site, there are clues that the old river may have washed away the lower enclosure bank

    An old Hampshire farmer told me of old haystacks where a small place was kept clear in the centre. It was probably for basic maintenance of the tabernacle and accrued special value from that. Was this the origin of another name associated with mazes, Shepherd's Bower? Maybe due to symbolism Salisbury Cathedral was built on top of sheep bones. Another farmer told me of how he and his father used  to lay dry sticks flat on the ground beneath the haystack to assist in the aeration and prevent overheating. Drainage and aeration was further improved by the excavation of a ditch, initially perhaps a spiral but eventually someone, a sentient being, devised what we call the classic maze. It has a unique internal symmetry not known anywhere else in Nature. It caught on worldwide. As they moved into autumn, people fed off the fruits of the trees and the cattle grazed the grass. Then in October time they had their first weaning from that which was stacked finally between the halo and the halos. This led to Halloween. Ween is to do with 'expectation and hope'.

The winter passed and the food store was depleted. How? Well, maybe we can imagine the original use of Stonehenge. Those who had earlier brought their straw turned up on the avenue and approached the henge. There by the heoul stone stood the boss of the site. The visitor checked in and then went to the stack and withdrew a share of food. He was then relieved of one or more of his corn dollies. This was the original credit card and one can imagine clever people running a stook exchange. The stook being the name for a specific volume of straw. Stook, stock? Basically a generally agreed measure. Small stones may have been used as doles and this is the early basis of measuring set amounts. The Greek for small stones is calculus.

As the stack became smaller, the riggbands were moved inwards, attaching to smaller circles of riggbols.

There are records of cattle being carried to the haystack at the end of the winter in Sweden. In some cases, nearby enclosures close to the haystacks would have been overwintering grounds for stock considered worthy of taking through the winter. Thus the wasting of energy driving cattle would have been prevented. Pigs are more difficult to move and they can fatten quickly on a wider range of vegetative material, including the twigs of the bolraces, so they would have been a preferred creature for local butchering carried out within the henge areas. Pigs also consume human effluent.

Some henges had an adjacent enclosure where stock, often pigs, were kept so they could be fed more easily and periodically slaughtered through the winter as part of the doling out process. Stooks gave way to bales, so a bail-out sometimes happened. Bones and other remains were boiled in cauldrons and this was another part of the doling out.

If when the populace saw THE LAST STRAW they looked around and saw all the new little points in full growth they knew they had calculated right and that they would have several seasons of relatively trouble-free life ahead of them. The Spring was with them. If there were any doubts, they would fast just to make sure they would survive. The mechanism of fasting must have led to many surviving who otherwise would not. So the Lenten fast is based on practicality.

As agriculture developed, the thrashing was done by man and beast and later the man stood on a board with stones (shards) embedded in its base. He holds a goad as held by the Goddess Neith.
The threshold remained. See the height of the stooks.

A more sophisticated device with roller emerged later

If the grass was growing again, they could put the cattle out to graze and they would celebrate not just that the new May had come but that they had survived as a group and individually. Before the fun could start another task was in hand namely capturing thousands of rats that had decided to shelter under the haystack. Dogs helped with this but there are records of the numbers being so great that the natural aggressive skills of the dogs were exhausted and they looked on whilst the rest were dealt with by man. The rats were hit with sticks. The carcasses were buried in more recent times but there is every possibility in earlier times that they were eaten. Rigid sticks have long been used for clouting and killing rats (priests) and everyone involved would have had one. I am wondering whether a remnant of this has found its way into Morris Dancing. Look at meaning of letters in Appendix and hints at why we call a RAT, a RAT.

The riggbands hung loose and a dance was derived around that. The maypole dance allows a group of people to stand as individuals each connected to the male pole and the female earth by a riggband. They were bound together, the root of the concept of destiny. They knew all were connected by a common thread and it was another thread called a 'clew' that allowed the hero Theseus to find his way in and out of the labyrinth. He would not have needed a clue if the Minotaur were in a maze.

All the ropes and hangers in the modern theatre are still called clews and in the earliest days of theatre sailors, familiar with the rigging and clews on ships, were employed to ensure the show went on.

The dancers then, by a commonly agreed procedure, clad the ridgepole and wrapped it round. Round and round or Troija another maze connection. The ribbons now used are totally impractical for retaining straw in high winds and the coloured nature of later ribbands was for peripheral symbolic use, in the same way that Coca Cola turned a green man into a red and white Father Christmas. They danced the righeoul (the reel) and thousands of riggadoon dances (rig adorn) and in many cases over the rigoll. Is this the origin of groovy dances?

What connection between the heoul stone at Stonehenge and the heoul in righeoul? This set of highly developed agricultural dances succeeded a much wider range of nature-related dances such as those associated with the arrival of the cranes. Geranos, the crane dance heralded another key time in their uncalendraical year. The primitive agriculture was fading away but many of the ancient rites were kept by the migrant seasonal workers we now call gypsies. If the site had a rigoll cut

INTENSE EXTERNAL ENERGY

ENTERS OUR REALITY

THE EARTH SUBSTANTIAL

into the ground, they would have had the original groovy dances in the dance hals.

The maypoles have all but gone and grain can be bought in bags from Pets at Home or SCATS or we buy flour or ready-made bread. Many of the high places were deemed remote and too dry to grow crops so they were planted with Beech Trees as they provided the healing wood used in sheep dips, so the sheep did not get foot rot.

One symbolic person remains from those times and it is the person who sought to celebrate that central pole, not even the earlier tree, with his body. From his trunk and limbs hang the riggbands, he stamps and leaps and in his hands he carries symbols of the riggbols, the pieces of wood that ringed around the maze kept the straw in place and maybe the priests used to kill rats. Maybe he wears bells emulating the resounding bells in sistrums, used to frighten away birds or later the gongs that hung in the trees in the sacred grove of Dodonna, that high windswept place that reminded us of the useful power of the wind in the winnowing process and as the natural engine of sailing ships. Dodonna's sacred grove where the wind blowing and chiming in evidence of that winnowing force led to the invention of church bells and prayer wheels.

Church bells did not just call people to prayer they were the first prayers and the prayers were engraved on the bells. The message of the Morris Man is engraved more subtly in his appearance and his dress.

Symbology has therefore been built upon various practical tool and dynamics that contribute to physical survival.

So we should not think of the three things the Goddess is seen here holding as symbols of her power but clues to what is needed outside one's self to ensure survival, a flail, a goad and a shepherd's crook.

Other complicated symbolic activities took place and these were based on another basic tool the sistrum. It was used to get sheep and birds to move where one wanted them or simply to frighten crows or other predators away.

One of these is African and one is Egyptian.

What of the female Moeris dancer? The ancients knew that all men have female in them and all women have male in them. Rarely do they cross with animals but they did once and that was when the wife of MIN *O S* mated with a bull TAURUS and a bi-generic hybrid resulted MIN (the male) *O* (The female) and Taurus (The Bull). Minotaurus. MINOS was named symbolically. He was to be associated with Special Forces like any acknowledged King, so the first part of his name referred to MIN, the ithyphallic fertility god of the Egyptians (and earlier). The ancients knew that genetically all males had some female in them and vice versa, so he has an *O* representing the birthing aspect and then an *S* which referred to him being of the flesh.

MIN was a brilliant model. He is seen with an exaggerated phallic organ, his head and hands black to represent the fertile mud of the Nile Delta and he is carrying a flail ready to create on-going provender from the crop. Another important agricultural device is behind him goading him and you can see it in some of the old images of agriculture.

The Goddess Neith carried one also and it is the goad. The rod was used to goad the cattle into pulling the plough and the thrashing board in the best direction. Its size gave rise to ancient and still-used measures.

I am trying to goad you into thinking differently about the direction you take when thinking about mazes and labyrinths.

The boat hook is almost identical and that has remained unchanged for thousands of years simply because its function has not changed and the design has to be simple to work.

In this Indian symbology, the halo effect at the top of the dedal is emphasised by the sun's rays, the rays being the beams that find their way into our existence. Most do not.

The Mayan example shows a productive female

being the roots of a productive tree and another hint at the special astrological alignments employed in certain henges.

The ancients had lots of stories to fill their spare time and many of them never found a way into the written tradition. Doing the right thing was an important topic and so, one story tells you or reminds you what might happen if you go against the will of the gods. King Minos, note a symbolic name, MIN for the male, O for the female and S for the living flesh, was given a very superior bull and the reason he was given it was for him to immediately sacrifice it to Poseidon to have him prove that he considered himself a lesser-being than the gods and that one in particular.

He looked at the bull and saw the opportunity of crossing it with his own cattle bringing personal benefit rather than honouring the gods.

From that moment on, the story reveals how a selfish approach can lead to undesirable outcomes. We do not know the detail of his agricultural endeavours but one story is his wife became so entranced with the powerful, beastly, male-force that she sought to seduce it. There's nothing wrong with lust if it is harnessed correctly. Same with gust, good sails needed. It did not work as the bull was a bull and not interested in human beings. This left Pasiphae in a tricky situation and she needed help.

If she had wanted a sword, she would have called on one called smith. If she had wanted a cart, she would have called on one with a name associated with such specialist skills, namely Carter. She needed someone with access to special skills to do with the mysterious areas. There was someone working under the name of Daedalus. The name drew on the positive mystery associated with The Dedale.

If one looks at the detail, one might find reasons to suspect his validity.

Stories tell of him killing his nephew Talos because the boy had discovered the saw and invented compasses; he did not want competition. If Pasiphae had known this, she might not have employed Daedalus. As it proved, any association with Daedalus leads to trouble. His marketing was good, so she

commissioned him and he suggested that she commission him, for a fee of course, to produce a specially made wooden cow, clad in real cow-skin.

Here, he holds open the lid so she can climb in.

The bull was tricked into mating with her and the result was named MIN O Taurus, a bi-generic hybrid. Various artists have represented different aspects of the beastliness, some happy and some sad.

Sculptor Michael Ayrton

reflected the sadness associated with a lonely being, Picasso and Chagall the sexy aspect of the beast and in one of his later stain-glass works in Chichester Cathedral Marc Chagall alluded to the need to respect the beast in all of us in order to best control our lives as human beings. When the Minotaur was born after a period of gestation identical to normal babies, Minos must have been deeply embarrassed. Evidence proved he had gone against the wish of the gods and it was evident that his wife had not only had an external affair, but she had had it with a bull and the result, the Minotaur, was there for all to see. He needed help and the cunning Daedalus was to hand. It was an accepted part of life that if one wanted to affect 'change' then one meditated on it and one did this in the presence of a symbolic image. This was the symbol of quick change and it was called the **labrys**.

It was the double-headed axe and the butterfly, both agents of quick change. It was kept safe in a place with many rooms and passages called a **labyr**inth. So at no small cost, Daedalus had a labyrinth built and the minotaur was placed inside, hopefully in an attempt to change it back to something more normal.

It did not work. Minos was angry, understandably. There are many associated stories and one is that Icarus was born illegitimately to Daedalus. Could the boy be playing in the presence of Daedalus; Pasiphae and the artificial cow be Icarus and a child born to Pasiphae, the venture between Pasiphae and the Bull being something planned by Daedalus and Pasiphae during one of their earlier encounters? Maybe Pasiphae had asked Daedalus for a special bull and he was intercepted by Minos as he brought it to their home. "What's all this about?" asks Minos.

"Er… it's for you and you could sacrifice it to Poseidon, that would be good," says Daedalus, lying again.

Eventually, Theseus turned up, and he and Pasiphae's daughter, Ariadne, fell for each other.

She decided to help Theseus penetrate the labyrinth. If it had been a maze, the Minotaur would have escaped long before and he could just walk round until he got to the centre. It was not however a maze; it was a labyrinth.

As Pliny said, "Labyrinths, we must not compare this to what we see traced upon our mosaic pavements or to the mazes formed in the fields for the entertainment of children and thus suppose it to be a narrow path

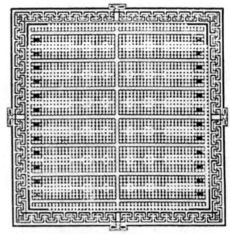

The Egyptian Labyrinth restored plan, Luigi Canina

132

along which we may walk for many miles together, but we must picture ourselves an edifice with many doors and galleries which mislead the visitor."

She gave him a thread and some stories reveal it was given to her by Daedalus. The thread, called a 'clew', unravelled and Theseus followed it to the centre where he found the Minotaur.

He slew the Minotaur and it went back in death to its three component parts, so Nature was back to normal. Minos had received an enormous bill for these wasted efforts so he put Daedalus and his son Icarus in the labyrinth, hoping perhaps that it would change his ways. Daedalus did have some skills and as before he put them to his own primarily selfish use.

Together with his son, they made some wings out of feathers and beeswax. They flew out of the labyrinth but the gods had been watching. The fate of Icarus was to be inspired, like many a youth, to fly fast and high and so as he got higher and higher, the oldest god of them all, Helios, the Sun, caused the wax to melt and the innocent Icarus plummeted to his death into the Aegean Sea and the arms of Poseidon. Poseidon got his own back and the message that one should not go against 'the will of the gods' was put across in a very moving way.

Many stories may have been lost. What if one of the early audiences asked, "How come wax and feathers were available? Did the Minotaur keep bees and chickens?"

In another story, Theseus was said to be the result of a beachside liaison involving Poseidon, so maybe Poseidon was sending a message to his son also.

There was a labyrinth at Lake Moeris and that was not a maze. A maze is one pathway. Pliny amongst others explains the differences and he asks us particularly not to confuse labyrinths with those things we find in mosaics and in the fields.

A labyrinth is complicated with lots of choices; it is not easy to find your way unless you know. Something special was kept there and that was the labrys. This was the double-headed axe of the Minoans. If we look closely at the axe we can see a clue to its practical use. The right-hand blade in such tools is sharper to enable trimming off of small branches before more force is applied by the left blade to chop the wood up. We can see the wear on the right blade. The late Marija Gimbutas, the American archeologist, has posed that this also represented the epiphany of the mother Goddess in the form of a butterfly. So they used insects to explore their psyche also but what makes the butterfly important and different from the male rigg? They both represent aspects of something they knew was one of the most important things in existence, **change**. So the tree was rigid, tough and inflexible through long periods of time and it was called a male name. The butterfly was transient emerging from a small chrysalis or cocoon, liquid inside if opened too early, but when the time is right a split is formed and red blood drops and out comes a form so different from the chrysalis. It pumps up its wings and then flies away, delicate, beautiful and feminine.

This symbology remained and was used in Christian symbology.

The cocoon body of the goddess reveals also a vagina shaped like an almond (Prunus amygdalus) and a Christ-child is being born from it.

OUR LADY OF   CHARTRES CATHEDRAL
WALSINGHAM, ENGLAND

The axe also represents a sudden act, soon started and soon finished.

Many flying things were considered bringers of oracular messages. How do I know? Again, little birdie told me.

So the dance is all to do with change and celebrating those aspects of it that we have control over to our benefit. A dance should be planned and social and it may have a fairly substantial requirement of stamina and persistence. It should be simple enough for all to learn so they can actively participate. What better way to forget the hardships of life than to transcend them in a changed state through the dance?

The riggboll in addition to be of great use holding the riggbands may have taken on a symbolic mode in the form of decoration. This one is from Africa.

Picture taken in California 2008

134

In July 2011, a charity I was chairman of employed a drummer who was dressed in an outfit from Africa. It was identical to our conventional mummers outfit with the ribbons or riggbands. Dirk Campbell has discovered links between the Celtic knot patterns and ancient music. The plot unfolds.

I may be contributing to my 'tea pot theory' but the image shown on the carved stone above reminds me of someone else!

This is the domestic Egyptian God who was always shown facing one. Every home had one of these. He grinned. If a child was seen smiling in its sleep, they said it was because it had seen Bes in its dreams. It was a god that represented 'the bringing in of goodness'. The *T* on the end of BEST alludes to the great substance. "Tell me to a *T*," we still say.

ALL THE **BEST** TO YOU.

One other thing that is still the same is that we tend to dwell away from places of industry, perhaps where it is more sheltered or there is a source of water.

In the times of the giant haystacks, the places people lived were based on the same model.

They did not live in the Dol Haus but in a smaller place of similar design usually on lower ground.

The Dolhaus was very similar to the ordinary house.

Perhaps one of the most important things we should absorb and try to acknowledge is that early man was very intellectual. The Classic Type One Maze as we call is universal and whilst it does the job as a rigoll or drain under ancient haystacks it was used because its design fascinated everyone. It is no more practical than a simple helix.

We can now say it has 'internal rotational symmetry'. It does not matter whether the design is circular or rectangular the inherent internal rotational symmetry lies within.

So far as I know, it does not exist in any living thing. Other mathematical dynamics like Fibonacci and various other spirals are common but the Type 1 Classic Maze design came out of the head of some creative human being. The Roman amphitheatres are based on Fibonacci and Shostokovich based music on the Fibonacci series. Sir John Tavener used sacred geometry in his compositions. What about old dances?

The practical function has gone, so we are left with a vague fascination and this is based on an inner knowledge that it refers to something very important.

This leads me to another area to do with man's understanding. The word understanding is a clue. In his earliest intellectual understandings, he tuned into basic things like being and various relative realities. Somehow he was able to embrace the Earth and celebrate his sense of being by placing things and joining things in special ancient harmonies. These places became libraries of consciousness, reminders and celebrations of the mysteries from which they gained some sort of understanding about their position and perhaps their role in the manner of things.

The private prayer, the sung hymn is transient. Many of the symbols made from wood soon erode in this reality. Even things made from stone are lost due to earthquakes, flooding and re-use for other purposes. They are not conserved as man's presence and interest moves away from them.

Places like the Pyramids and Stonehenge have clues to underlying dynamics of this reality and maybe clues to other realities. These were included in the design of these large-scale features as well as in the design of smaller artefacts each with their own function in this reality.

So from a beginning where wooden poles allowed men to plot the progress of the Sun and Moon for agricultural processes and helping with warehouse management through the winter, we see an honouring of these dynamics in stone. The original riggbols would have been wood as is hinted at at Woodhenge, but perhaps later larger stones between the rings of smaller threshold stones. In the presence of exceptional wealth of resources and creativity grand designs like Stonehenge emphasised the importance of Nature's forces at very high and sometimes obscure levels.

Some of the assets of places like this are still available and we need to subscribe to them to bring back into our consciousness dynamics that will facilitate our being and reaching into mysterious futures with safety.

The Romans developed a series of Priestly Lords and they were basically focused on job descriptions.

- **Vervactor**, "He who ploughs"
- **Reparator**, "He who prepares the earth"
- **Imporcitor**, "He who ploughs with a wide furrow"
- **Insitor**, "He who plants seeds"
- **Obarator**, "He who traces the first plowing"
- **Occator**, "He who harrows"
- **Serritor**, "He who digs"
- **Subruncinator**, "He who weeds"
- **Messor**, "He who reaps"
- **Conuector** (Convector), "He who carries the grain"
- **Conditor**, "He who stores the grain"
- **Promitor**, "He who distributes the grain"

Key is **the caring attendance of all mankind regardless of race or creed**. In fellowship absorbing communally, personally and with some sense of wonder dynamics that cannot be changed or controlled. They have to be accepted and ideally celebrated.

The origins of conventional mazes go back way into the past but a man who died 2nd Dec 2005, aged ninety-six, **Randoll Coate**, initiated what we now call the Modern Symbolic Maze. They are mostly labyrinths but the new concept was the inclusion of pictorial images with sometimes many levels of meaning, some obvious and some hidden. Whilst they do not enrich modern agriculture, they powerfully enrich the deep levels of man's intellect and it is upon that inner power that we have based our successful evolution on this planet. The Modern Symbolic maze was preceded by puzzle mazes some of which were hedges and the early ones we call Type-2 Mazes could be solved by putting ones hand on a hedge wall and keeping it there as one walked. Eventually one reached the centre. Then a clever man, an eminent eighteenth-century mathematician, **4th Earl Stanhope**, invented a design The Type-3 Maze where if one did that you ended up back at the beginning. Mazes became places of entertainment.

These modern designs have one thing in common with the ancient mazes and that is 'the span' the regular spacing between one barrier and the next. It will vary according to the measure of access needed whether it be a finger following a track of mosaic or a family tramping along a wide pathway.

Labyrinths can be any size and if one considers fife to be a labyrinth, size-less.

In a labyrinth, 'dead-ends' are not a problem; without them it would not be a labyrinth.

So perhaps the ideal is to think one is at a goal even if it is a dead end. This should not remove the hope for more and to enjoy the Tantalus that sometimes draws one nearer to it.

A key mystery is to do with the massive weight and size of certain constructions and whilst we have the essential need to feed people with food and the long established systems for achieving this have been in place, there are two other dynamics. One is to do with knowledge about **astronomical alignments and measures** and powers to move very heavy things.

On the edge of our understanding we are tempted by the possibilities of levitation and extra-terrestrial intelligences.

Man has always subscribed to grandeur but the scale of it in communities where life was very simple at a basic level is very tantalising.

The Bankh at Figsbury Ring

In some cases, the central henge was surrounded by a deeply excavated ditch and this may have been in place for two reasons. One, a steep-sided Ha Ha to control the movements of cattle, store cattle, grain or perhaps a water-filled moat for water supply

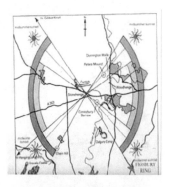

The Classic Type-1 maze has existed for thousands of years and its early use was a functional drainage gully beneath the haystack. It then linked to symbolism and entertainment in the form of dancing.

The puzzling concept fascinated man, so a new form of

DANEBURY RINGS

entertainment was introduced with hedge mazes. The Type-2 labyrinth had junctions but if you kept your hand on the sidewall, it led you to the centre. The Type-3 labyrinth was designed so that if you kept your hand on the wall, you ended up back at the entry.

Then Randoll Coate came up with the concept of The Modern Symbolic Labyrinth, more complex in respect of the journey but full of images tuned into a particular topic. Extremely clever and creative thinking! His maze imprint tuned into the Minotaur and if one applies the scale of the footprint to the rest of the body, the Minotaur would be as tall as the Eiffel Tower in Paris, one of Randoll's favourite cities.

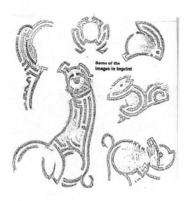

The client was Scottish, so a Scotty Dog and the frog at the top alludes possibly to Randoll's name. RANA is the frog and he is DOLING out something.

Lord Bath's favourite maze at Longleat is The Labyrinth of Love.

The surface meaning Pradash looks like a traditional historic landscape and fits in with the old house.

However, it has many levels of meaning and connected with love and passion.

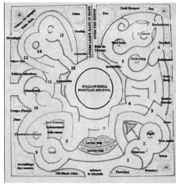

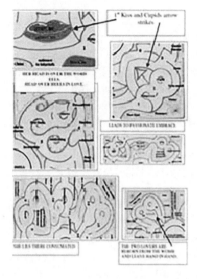

So curvaceous lines tune into meanings in a graphic way and they are assembled along a time line of experience, so it becomes a story.

Part of wedding celebrations

So it is all about searching for the basic intuits underlying the words and other linear configurations like drawing. Earlier, we mentioned the Egyptian punt. Well, it is driven not just by the men sitting on the bankh, an essential contributor is the wind and the device that harnesses the energy of the wind whether it be extreme gusts or breezes is what we still call the sail. The uprights in hurdles are also called sailles and there used to be ten in each hurdle, possibly linking to the fingers on the hand. The botanists have tuned into an old name for the Willow, Saille and it is scientifically referred to now as Salix. One can see how a willow responds positively to gusts of wind. So, all is to do with something that can harness external forces to bring benefit to humankind. Your Willows at Giverny Claude harness your love gusts.

The hurdle harnessed livestock by keeping them in, or keeping them out.

A later use of Salix was tuning into the acetylsalicylic acid, aspirin.

So another form of healing or heouling?

Why Salisbury is called Salisbury?

The number of uprights in a basic woven fence panel made of hazel or willow is ten. Fingers on hand?

Each upright, straight rod is called a **SAILLE.** The old name for Willow is **SAILLE** and the new scientific Latin name is **Sal**ix.

There is a record of an article one hundred and forty-five-plus years ago in *The Andover Advertiser* of a fence being put round a haystack after the crop had been removed and terriers put in to kill the rats. A similar fence may have been put round the haystack to keep grazing animals out when the haystack was full of the harvested crop after thrashing in THE HALOS or thrashing floor. Organised groups **SALLIED** to do the work. **So a constructed device to help hold the productive crop in place.** The Egyptian punt also has **SAILS** but in that case, they exist to harness the gusts of wind to create a productive end-result, a journey with produce in THE HOLD in THE HULL.

Those **SAILS** also had an interesting set of components that help solve the problem of harnessing the gusts, namely CLEWS. In the days of the early theatres, e.g. at the Globe by the River Thames, local fishermen were employed to raise the curtains and move other parts of the sets and the gear used is still called the CLEWS. A clue is A MEANS OF SOLVING A DIFFICULTY. On the ship, the sailor's actions were controlled by whistles. This was why

whistling in the audience was banned in theatres later as it might have led to scenery being moved at the wrong time, resulting in injury to performers.

The old haystacks were storage areas built over the THRESHOLD and this is where the words BURY and BARROW come from. A BURRWALL was the name given to a slope beside a bank; it helped contain. Salisbury was surrounded by very productive agriculture. If all effectively applied, the **SAILOR** or THE **SALES**MAN could apply **SELL**ING skills. On the Egyptian punts the men rowing sat on what was called the bankh.

Now when a ship has to lower its mast the point of union between mast and hul is called the tabernacle. All tied in with BANKHING and STOOK EXCHANGE.

So **SALIS**BURY was and is a place with many **SAILLES**BURYS the basis of a local economy and also a WHOLE **SAILLE** ECONOMY.

An early form of celebration was WAS **SAILL**ING (old English was hal and the hal refers to the thrashing floor, halos in Greek). So, a place of healing.

Ves heill in Nordic = be healthy. Heoul Stone at Stonehenge?

One way we have tuned into underlying networks is leylines and this was applied to the positioning of special halls or churches. *A* refers to our perceived reality and the name Michael has *M* for nurturing; *I* for being one; *C* capable of creation and then the universal aspirant *H*, then *A* for our perceived reality; then *E*, capable of taking in holding and giving out energies and information and *L* relating to underlying spiritual energies.

These special churches may have been placed at special ANGLES, so many are called St Michael and The Angels. So look at things from different angles?

Marliac

It was a warm morning and the soft bloom on the purple plums tells the story of autumn coming and harvest. In a warm town in the south of France, a ten-year-old boy sits in his father's library. Around him in the fields, the haystacks warm in the hot sun. The only one who would maybe paint them, Claude Monet, will soon be born in Paris in the eleventh month. There was such a wonderful library full of his father's oldest books and his father's latest book on the local flora. Around him, all the classical heroes, gods and goddesses, older families with old, old stories all for the telling, all were waiting for someone to tell us. The oldest story or stories is the one by Nostradamus another Frenchman with some things to say in many ways, in a green language of his own.

The boy sits still in the library of wooden shelves with the paper in the books filled with stories. The stories that interest him most are the ones that whisper, just to him, perhaps.

He does want to tell some of the stories but he is honouring the sensitivity of their making and his discovery of the sounds. I will tell you now he has learned all their names these old gods and goddesses and he has walked where they walked. He has listened close by the Omphalos and knows about all the other omphali and heard the ancient stories of the universe. The geometry connects with a special transition of Venus.

When he started his serious classical studies in Toulon at the age of eleven, he was already familiar with his topic and it was no surprise when he gained an MA at a young age. We are not told what he learned of Sumer, whether they knew of the Omphalos before these stones, destined to lose all light to become black, landed in meteoric splendour on the planet that they named 'Earth' and which to them meant 'Faraway Place'. It may be a story to be told from the old shelves of some library somewhere. Maybe you will tell us.

Sitting in the warming sun here in the south, he is far from the Paris he left when the new surges of energy lapped up against the walls of the University in 1848.

He returned to the warm south in readiness for a great undressing prior to a great sexual exploration. He thought he was escaping from something he did not understand, something that he was afraid of, something he could not handle alone without the enveloping life of the countryside. That is why he left Paris, maybe.

He married amongst the plums and haystacks at the age of twenty-two years, twice the cyclic number of the sun and in the church at Temple Sur Lot maybe. He moved to that little town to help the plums and the almonds mature each autumn. **The almond** is Prunus amygdalus alluding to the Magdeline and the ovarian shape of the Almond seed. This man is Bory La Tour Marliac.

He loved his garden and the sacred lotuses that reminded him of the gardens of Egypt and the life of the ancient god and goddess. At twenty-eight years of age, he read. He was always reading something or other, an article by Georges Leveque in Revue Horticole. "What a pity!" it said, "That the hardy Nymphaeas do not exist in such a variety of colours as the tropical ones." So as in any of these mysterious stories you have only to ask 'why' in the right place and the right moment, to be caught by the gods and the goddesses.

You may be given a task. For him, they were sitting in their library waiting for a knock on their consciousness, or should I say their combined consciousness. The knock is often that special letter we write as *W*. So many doors are opened by its signal sound when placed at the door of words like what, when, why, who, why, which and where. If you thought it was weird, they would probably agree wholeheartedly.

"Why are there no coloured Nenuphar rustiques?"

"Would it be a better place if there were?" He did not know the answer to the first question but he was sure they would be a beautiful addition to the Earth.

We might ask why he not leaved well alone. Why cut into the natural forest? Why cut down the great tree? Why sow the seed and reap the harvest? Why stack it in the fields to turn golden? Below the dark mud of the Euphrates, Tigris and even the Tiber in quieter places the submerged root waits for the spring as it always waited for spring. It was there before the Pharaohs and the golden-tipped pyramids. Then from the primordial filth, it strikes out green spikes leaves and finally glorious flowers in blue, white and pink. It is a symbol appearing lit by light. Its appearance reminds us of the light.

The task began and the first steps were into science. This is a scientific story, so I am keeping it simple and uncoloured, though the search was for colour. It was understood by a man called Weisman that inheritance had something to do with a thing he called the Id. It was carried in pollen in male flowers and seeds in female flowers. The Ids led the plants to manifest in their various forms in the light. Research showed that the Id for whiteness of flower petals was present in the common white water lily of Europe. One other colour existed and that was red which had come from a mutation grown in Zurich. This had been named <u>Nymphaea Froebeli.</u>

144

Now the habit of the water lily, a submerged resting rootstock that threw up aquatic leaves that float on the surface, later to be followed by flowers is not confined to any one continent. Marliac discovered through his contacts a wider range of colours spread across the globe.

He conversed with the experts of the day. William Robinson, the Father of English Flower Gardening met him on one of his journeys down through France and they became friends. William Falconer was another, an ex Kew Gardens man who went to Gunnersbury House near Kew where the first imported plant of Nymphaea odorata, the American Pink, flowered. Falconer was to go onto Schenley Park in the USA where he furthered his own interest in the Nymphaeas. Marliac subsequently named red lilies after both these men. Over the years, he visited various countries and collected the full genetic range, bringing samples and their Ids back to Temple Sur Lot.

From America, he brought the wonderful large pinks and whites of the odoratas and tuberosas, from Mexico the yellow of Nymphaea mexicana and from Japan, Nymphaea tetragona, a smaller species.

Attempts to make them cross had been made before and all had failed, so Marliac turned to the science of reproduction. Everything he did, he did in secret. Finally he achieved success by combining old practices and applying it to his project. It was eleven years before he had sufficient confidence to start bulking up his new progeny and five years later he set up his nursery at Temple Sur Lot.

The story of the Nymphaeas has been told and retold many times and the first time I heard it I took it at face value. Many asked Marliac how he had succeeded in his work No one ever found out how he did it. However, he revealed everything but in the form of a rebus a code. All was heard but little was understood.

Why I should be the only person to twig what he was about I do not know? Why I should have trained in botanical ways at Kew **Pic Palmhouse** and run the lily pond as part of my responsibility in Arboretum South and why I should end up running Longstock the finest water garden in Europe? Why I should gradually move upstream to my spring fed home is more of a mystery. **Pic Longstock**

It bathed me in water lilies and their names and it was the names that seemed strange. It is weird that all human kind prefers to call things by two names. The conflict between need and limitation distils our everyday usage down to two words. Arm chair, grocers shop, paintbrush and most of our friends are given binomial description. All living things known to science have been given binomial names in Latin. Some of the names are descriptive to help us remember them and some names recur. Marliac was a plantsman with a foot in Botanical circles and another in the fancy flower trade. So he made up names for the water lilies he bred. The true Botanist by profession would never look at the fancy water lilies as a group, so he never came across Marliac's names. The general gardener uses both fancy and true botanical names but the botanical names just might as well be fancy as he or she generally does not understand their wider purpose in accurate botanical nomenclature. So long as the plant can be specified, bought and sold, discussed and enjoyed, they are happy. So with came across these names.

I asked, "Why?"

They, the Gods were waiting for the question and by this time Marliac was beside them.

I will ask you now to make this man happy and listen to his story again and then tell the story to others.

When he saw that he was having some success with his crossings, he decided he needed to tell the story and make some sort of cogent record for his own use.

For his own satisfaction, he had made his breeding ponds in the shape of a womb or a plant ovary. Around these, he placed hundreds of terracotta pots in which he placed his special soil and the seeds he had gathered from the collected lilies. **Pic Marliac ponds**

But what is anything without a name, to be silently known by, a name to be called by; a name to celebrate; a name to imply a family, a name to describe a face or way of facing, a signpost to guide us onwards in the light.

He had to make some names, some new names arising from the new births and the evolutions of his story. In his story, he had to tell us several stories so he made various types of names and he made them code names. He chose two-part names and made them up installing the number three, trisyllabic to draw our attention.

In his great rebus, he compiled names describing his technique of placing the stock plants in water made acid with oak gall, also starving the plants as the ancients did their cattle to induce greater fecundity and touching the male organs and their pollen with a horsehair brush before transferring it to the female stigma.

Great scientists and collaborators are celebrated in his new names so are Native American Indian Tribes in celebration of the union between the North American Lilies; the Mexican Lilies and the European Lilies. Sexuality is alluded to in the names of the Gods and Goddesses and their natural habitats.

His nursery sat upon springs and he called it his boat. He even named a lily Le Bateaux.

Camille was eleven years old and Monet was twenty-nine when Marliac started to make his crosses.

In 1877, Marliac released **Nymphaea carnea** alluding to the rosy, fleshy fingers of the new dawn. Indeed, the sun was rising on a new generation. The sun was flooding in and from the space he had made many new seedlings saw the light and grew towards it.

In 1887, **Nymphaea Equiseta**. (Exquisite yes, but also Equus and setae, horse and bristle). Over the next few years, more good pinks emerged but in 1881, a palindromic year, he released one of his most wonderful plants. He called it **Chromatella** (Chroma = colour, Tella, the bull). Out of the watery fields came the golden yellow lily. It was a cross between Nymphaea odorata x

Nymphaea mexicana and possibly Nymphaea alba. No one asked why he named it so.

> For whom dost thou sing?
> For whom dost thou fill thy mouth with songs?
> Man is deaf; he does not hear
> He is blind he does not see
> And has no perception?
> Later, he brought pure oil
> With it he anointed the horns of Serisu the Bull
> He plated with gold the tail of **Tella**, the bull.

From the second tablet of the 'Song of Ullikummis' where the great wave asked Ishtar.

In 1899, Marliac won prizes at the Grand Exposition in Paris. The man who would paint these lilies was banned from the exposition. **Pic Marliac lilies**

Flammea was after the Roman priests [the **Flammen** who wore the woollen cap of office (the apex and priesthood) with the olive stick protruding from the top]

Tell again the story of the golden store of hay and the lambskin cover but change the tale. **Aurora** after the Goddess of the Dawn, the between time, **Ellisiana** after Ellis the district where Olympia stood or later lay; liceae is also a barrier or red herring, **Gloriosa** the combination of Aureola with Nimbus (the goddess in the morning sky and reflected in the waters nearby). Tell me the story of the forest and fieldside dawn. **Lucida**, shining, easily understood, **Purpurata**. Ate Goddess of mischief; **Seignouretii** (male Lord, eaterio a Botanical term for the seedcase); **Arc en ciel** = arcanum, mystery... Iris, the rainbow.

Ignea = first fire. His first red.

Colossea. Colossus name for Apollo. **Gracillima**, slender hairs, limus the mud.

Graziella. Graze = scrape ella = the gall. Scrape the gall to make the water acid. Technique described in the Millers Dictionary of Gardening, which was on his desk together with books by William Robinson and Mrs Richmond.

Hermosa = Herm (Greek) osage = orange of Oaklahoma; Mt Ossa and Hermes god of science.Hermetic= sealed and secret.

Paul Heriot = best beast, heriot is base fellow (O Fr).

As time passed, he despaired his secret would not be shared but he would not openly declare it. He hinted more in names like **Solfatare**. Solfa a system of syllables; sol = a solution to a difficulty tar = a lie, fata = a mirage.

He described how he had carved in the brick on the walls of the old farmhouse chickenhouse a number of runic marks recording his crosses. **Nymphaea Masaniello**

Mas = an old farmhouse. Niello = carving in relief. Mason = one who carves.

Vesuve the Roman Goddess of the hearth Vesta. Uva = a grape.

Commanche and **Sioux** celebrate Native American Indian tribes. The lilies combine the white and yellow of American species to give orange yellows.

Odalisque was the female slave of the harem =a female seed parent

Somptuosa = soma the body; Somptu = the sumptuary law.

Escarboucle = a mythical gem shining with a light from within. The carbuncle. His best red.

Galatee = galla the oak apple galate = salt or gallic acid.

Phoebus = the sun god;

Livingstone = explorer;

Hermes; thrice greatest god of science;

Again he tries to reveal with **Amabilis** = a from = Mab Queen of the Faeries.

Sultan = sul = sun tannin= oak bark; Tannin = dragon of the sea.

Venusta = Goddess of Love patron of gardeners.

Lusitania = Lusi Portugal; Tan =oak; Lucina = Juno; Tania = Faerey Queen.

Eucharist = Sacraments of Lords Supper = Eu = well charis = goddesses.

Then towards the end **Fabiola**. Fable or myth; IO invocation of triumph or grief. Another clue for us to question.

Arethusa = Guido of Arezzo; Aretinian syllables; Hus = House and USA

Gonnere. = Gr generation or seed; Nereid daughter of sea god; ere = heir.

Neptune = Roman sea god.

Marliac died in 1911, aged eighty-one years and for the next three years plants named in his code emerged. The last was **Rene Gerard** in 1914. The baton floated down the stream of time and a painter picked it up. This was the year Monet started to paint the Nymphaeas.

After that date with the author of the codes dead and still holding his secret, the basis of new names changed. Undoubtedly, some of the later releases were bred by Marliac but did not flower in his lifetime, so he could not name them.

In the thirteen years between Marliac releasing his first new hybrid and Monet planting up Giverny Marliac released twelve new varieties, seventeen before Monet first planted the pool.

The total number of new cultivars raised by Marliac is not really known but it approaches one hundred. They are grown all over the world.

What is the message in all of this? Two Frenchman or if you wish three with Nostradamus. Three Galls to add to the pot, each hiding so much from public opinion, keeping something special safe, wrapping it up for the future and revelation to you at this special time when we need to know.

BORY LA TOUR MARLIAC AND THE WATER LILY NAMES.		
	1875	Marliac founded nursery at Temple sur Lot
EQUISETA	1878	EX = OUT OF
		EQUI = HORSE (HORSE HAIR USED IN CROSSING)
		SETA= BRITSLE
		QUARERRE = TO SEEK
HELVEOLA	1879	HELVETIC = SWISS WATER PLANT NURSERY IN ZURICH
		HEL GODDESS OF DEAD
		OLA= A POT
SULFUREA	1879	SUL= ANCIENT WATER GOD
		EA= CREATOR OF MAN
		BABYLONIAN GOD OF DEEP
ROSEA	1879	RHODODACTYLOS HOMERS EPITHET
		ROSY FINGERS OF THE DAWN
ALBIDA	1880	ALB = WHITE
		ID = WEISMANNS THEORY ELEMENT IN CHROMOSOME CARRYING GENETIC MATERIAL
		MOUNT IDA IN CRETE
CHROMATELLA	1881	CHROMA COLOUR, MA = MOTHER
		TELLUS BUL OR ROMAN EARTH GODDESS
		ELLA = GALL
		ELLA = ROOT
		Epic of Gilgamesh. "And he gilded the tail of Tella the bull"

CARNEA	1887	FLESHY
SULPHUREA GRANDIFLORA	1888	Monet ordered 1894
RUBRA PUNCTATA	1889	DOTTED PUNCTURED
LAYDECKERI ROSEA	1892	Laydeckeri family name
		Monet ordered in 1894
GRACILLIMA ALBA	1893	GRACILUS = SLENDER
		CILIA = HAIRS
		LIMUS = MUD
IGNEA	1893	TO TAKE FIRE – FIRST REAL RED
ROSEA	1893	ROSY
PERFECTA	1893	THOROUGHLY DONE
L. FULGENS	1893	SHINING (RED)
L. LILACEA	1893	BLUISH
SEIGNOURETTI	1893	SEIGNOUR = LORD
		ETAERIO = GROUP OF DRUPELS OR ACHENES
FLAMMEA	1894	FLAMMEN ROMAN PRIEST
		FLAMM = FLAME
		EA = A RIVER also EAU
FULVA	1894	TAWNY DULL YELLOW
		AB = FROM
LAYDECKERI LUCIDA	1894	LUCID = SHINING
		EASILY UNDERSTOOD
		LUCINA ROMAN GODDESS CHILDBIRTH
		IDA MOUTAIN IN GREEC
SANGUINEA	1894	BLOODY
L. PURPURATA	1894	ATE = GREEK GODDESS OF MISCHIEF
		PURPORT?

ANDREANA	1895	ANDRE = MAN ANA-UP (Greek)
ROBINSONIANA	1895	After William Robinson father of English Flower Gardening
		He visited.
AURORA	1895	GODDESS OF DAWN
ELLISIANA	1896	ELL = CHROMATELLA?
		ISU = DESCENDED FORM
		ANA = AGAIN
		ELYSIAN = LOW LATIN A BARRIER
		ELLES = OTHERWISE
		OLYMPIA IN DISTRICTOF ELLIS
GLORIOSA	1896	RELIGIOUS SYMBOLISM
		Combination Aureola with Nimbus.
SPECIOSA	1899	SHOWY
SUAVISSIMA	1899	SWEET
ARC EN CIEL	1901	RAINBOW ARCANUM = MYSTERY
		EN = IN
		CIEL = UPPER LIMIT, CANOPY
WILLIAM FALCONER	1901	LEFT KEW 1872
		HEAD GARDENER IN KEY AREAS IN USA
		KEEN ON NYMPHAEAS
RICHARDSONII	1901	BRED N.tuberosa Richardsonii
COLOSSEA	1901	COL-NECK OSS = BONE
		APPLIED TO APOLLO
ATROPURPUREA	1901	ATROPUS-TURNING AWAY
		PURPLE.
		Darkest red. Monet bought one 1904
GRAZIELLA	1904	ELLA = THE ROOT. SCRAPE

		THE GALL.
HERMOSA	1904	HERM A HERALD
		OSAGE = OKLAHOMA
		HERMES = GOD OF SCIENCE
		MT OSSA
CHRYSANTHA	1905	GOLDEN FLOWER
PAUL HERIOT	1905	PAUL = LITTLE
		HERIOT = BEST BEAST
		HERLOT = BASE FELLOW O.F.
SOLFATARE	1906	SOLFA = SYSTEM OF SYLLABLES
		SOL = SOLUTION OF DIFFICULTY
		TAR = A FIB, A LIE
		FATA = A MIRAGE
VESUVE	1906	VESTA = ROMAN GODDESS OF THE HEARTH
		UVA = GRAPE
		EVA-EVE ET AL
ROSEA	1908	ROSY
COMMANCHE	1908	Honouring American breeders
SIOUX	1908	Honouring American breeders
ODALISQUE	1908	UDAL = WITHOUT FEUDAL SUPPORT
		FEMALE SKAVE OF HAREM
ROSITA	1908	ROSIT = RESIDUE OF TURPENTINE DISTILLATION.
		SIT-GREEK GRAIN OR FOOD.
		ROSETTA STONE
MASANIELLO	1908	MAS = MALE OR SMALL FARMHOUSE
		ONE WHO CUTS STONE/METAL
		NIELLO = ORNAMENTING BRICK BY ENGRAVING
ESCARBOUCLE	1909	MYTHICAL SELF-LUMINOUS

		GEM
		CARBONIC ACID, CARBUNCLE
DARWIN	1909	GENETIC FOCUS
GALATEE	1909	GALLA = OAK APPLE
		GALLATE = A SALT OR GALLIC ACID
		GALIPOT = TURPENTINE THAT EXUDES FORM CLUSTER PINE Fr.
		ATE = GODDESS OF MISCHIEF
LIVINGSTONE	1909	EXPLORER
FORMOSA	1909	SEE HERMOSA… HERM
		FORMOSA… FORM
		GLORIOSA… GLORI
		SPECIOSA… SPECI
		SOMPTUOSA… SOMPTU
PHOEBUS	1909	APOLLO SUN GOD
ATTRACTION	1910	ATTRACTING RED
CONQUEROR	1910	WINNER
HERMINE	1910	HERMES THRICE GREATEST
		THE GOD OF SCIENCE
NEWTON	1910	NEWTON
		NEW FASHION
		TONE
		MANNERS BREEDING
ALBATROSS	1910	FREEDOM TO BREAK THROUGH ESTABLISHED SYSTEMS OF KNOWLEDGE
MRS RICHMOND	1910	LADY WRITER… HER BOOK ON HIS DESK
LEVIATHON	1910	PRO-GENITOR OF LIFE
AMABILIS	1910	A = FROM
		MAB = QUEEN OF THE FAIRIES

		BRINGER OF DREAMS
VIRGINALIS	1910	GODDESS OF CHANGE AND LUCK
SULTAN	1910	SUL = SOL = SUN
		TAN = DIED 26th JAN 1911
		TANNIN = DRAGON OF SEA
SYLPHIDA	1910	A LITTLE SYLPH
		ID = AS BEFORE
		IDA = MOUNT IDA
	1911	**Latour-Marliac died 26th January, 1911**
METEOR	1912	METE = LATIN BOUNDARY OF SOLU
NOBILISSIMA	1912	HIGHER UNDERSTANDING
LUSITANIA	1912	LUSI = PORTUGAL
		TAN = OAK
		LUCINA = GODDESS JUNO
		TANIA = FAIRY QUEEN
GOLIATH	1912	BIG
EUCHARIST	1912	SACREMENTS OF THE LORDS SUPPER
		EU = WELL
		CHARIS = GODDESSES
ESMERALDA	1912	GENERATION ALLUDING TO POWER OF GREEN
INDIANA	1912	INDIAN
		DIANA ROMAN GODDESS
		IDENTIFIED WITH ARTEMIS
JAMES HUDSON	1912	HEAD GARDENER GUNNERSBURY PARK… FRIEND
VENUSTA	1912	GODDESS OF LOVE
		PATRON OF GARDENS
MARGUERITE LA PLACE	1913	

FABIOLA	1913	FABLE, MYTH
		IO = INVOCATIONTRIUMPH OR GRIEF
		OLLA = POT
GRAND TEMPLE SUR LOT	1913	

Chagall and Chichester

In the 1960s, the then Dean of Chichester Cathedral, Walter Hussey, a keen collector of fine art finally persuaded Marq Chagall the renowned artist to design a stain-glass window for the church. The commission was finally realised in October 1978.

Chagall was old, as was his client, and both men were sustained by the simple theme message: "Praise God in his holiness... Let everything that has breath praise the Lord."

In a communication sent on 22 May 1978, Charles Marq, the builder of the window, said, "I believe the property of every authentic work of art to contain **infinite possibilities of interpretation**."

What we see is the result of Marq Chagall applying very deep sensibilities going back to his Hassidic and country origins and a lifelong aspiration to spirituality.

Everyone sees things in their own way and I am going to tell you a story a little bit like the old troubadours; their stories had at least seven meanings. What follows is a prelude. I am reminded of when the late Derek Jarman visited a symbolic garden I had designed at the first Hampton Court Palace International Flower Show. He said, "You have designed a garden and we have come here to tell you stories about it."

Chagall was challenged. In one space, he had to encompass so much.

The obvious features in the window are the various small images celebrating Christian and Kristna dynamics. They are the culmination of the work and relate to the specific verses in the psalms. Every single figure of the congregation in the window is rejoicing by playing instruments or dancing or both. Most of the figures cannot be named but we can reasonably assume that the person at the very top, in respect of his kingly state, is King David.

The message is very obvious and that is that all can join in this celebration regardless of their faith. It is a message appropriate to a temple, a synagogue or a Christian church.

My belief is that the delay in the design process was due to a struggle to integrate the design in a powerful way. I was helped in my own personal understanding of their window by seeking an underlying design structure.

If you want to hang up your coat or coats, you seek a rack and there choose one or two hooks. One of the greatest tools ever made to aid spiritual thinking is the Cabballa or Tree of Life. It is not a real tree; it is a thinking model and a very sophisticated one.

The Cabballa can be hung on the cross bars or fenestration of the supporting framework and fits exactly three of them.

The cross bars of the Caballa support and importantly connect the spheres of thought that make up the Caballa.

There is another form of skeleton used by designers and this is sacred geometry. Like your own internal skeleton, it is common and it has been applied all over the world and specifically in temples to provide support. I have applied this discipline and two of the exercises produce interesting results. I was first looking for a Vesica Pisces. This is when two relevant circles overlap to produce a vesica in the centre. The design is commonly used throughout Christianity. You can even get a sticker for the back of your car. It is commonly used as a birthing symbol but I believe that in conjunction with the Cabbala symbol that lies within it. There is deep meaning and much to do with Jewish thinking. In some belief systems, the vesica pisces is male and female. Basically it refers to fertility and birthing.

So far we have a simple framework for complicated thought processes the Caballa and underlying geometries, one forming Vesica Pisces and another forming a Star of David. The latter encloses David on his steed.

I have applied another ancient model to the design and that is of The Minotaur. Chagall may have used this creature to put ourselves quite humbly into the picture.

The ancients knew that all men have female in them and all women have male in them. We have recently rediscovered this through genetics. In addition to our humanity, the ancients saw other forces some akin to the beasts around them. Some of our beastly ways are beneficent but some can be very difficult to control. Being close to a sheep, cow or donkey need not be worrying but being approached by a bull can be dangerous. Only by controlling the worst aspects of our inherent beastliness can we move to a higher state and ideally enter a spiritual state where we are free from all bodily limitations. I have the beast in me and recognise it. I see also The Minotaur a hybrid of male female and the bull. There are many stories about this imaginary concept.

This Minotaur is rather special, although morphologically it subscribes to the Attic tradition. It is kneeling and so in obeisance, perhaps prayer. There is no anger or oppressive action, but instead it is reaching into a pouch to sow seed. Hopefully the fertile seed will be sown, not into the stone floor at your feet but into a fertile mind, yours. The hand reaches into a purse shaped like the seedpod of Capsella bursa pastoris (The Shepherd's Purse). It is also the vesica Pisces of the sacred geometry and the fertile area designated Yesod in the cabbala.

The fact that it could be a reflection of ourselves is borne out by more clues. The seventh of the ten sefirot in the cabbala is Netzach and corresponds in the philosophy to the right leg. In the window it lays near the left leg of the Minotaur but if it is our reflection, it is our right leg. This suggests that whatever we see in the window, we should reflect on our own condition. So Claude and Ludwig, reflections again!

Netzach is also associated green with fields of green and indeed we see in this part of the window greener than anywhere else. Perhaps the small creature emerging out into the light is a vole. Some of the strange angles in this area of glass fit in with the angles of reflection when light passes into a raindrop. Maybe the glass experts had some fun with this.

On the opposite side Hod, which in the Cabbala relates to the left leg, is near the right leg of the Minotaur.

The Cabbala story is a deep one and I leave you to explore for the rest of your life.

There is the shape of another creature and one that formed an essential part of everyday life since time immemorial and that is the donkey. A friend of mine Sue Climpson first saw the donkey or half donkey that appears from the western side of the window. Our thinking is tested again. Is this the donkey that brought the Christian messiah heading back east, or is it one on its way to collect the Jewish Messiah?

Another friend Patrick Coggswell first saw a face and strangely it resembles in shape and posture a similar face in another of Chagall's works. It also resembles the 'turn-me-round' faces of Otto Weinberger a man who Chagall may have met in Paris. His work is all to do with looking at things in different ways.

As more attention has been focussed, various people have seen Bulls and lambs.

I see King David sitting on a less than anatomically accurate creature. I like to think of it as a sheep because when Hussey, Chagall and Marque made this window they were old and we are told in the scriptures that at the end of his active life King David returned to his sheep. The fact that he is riding side-saddle might remind us of earlier revered figures associated with creativity. He is at the top of the Cabballa and so closer to being out of this world and maybe that is where he is going.

One of the things that has already happened is that rather than people viewing the window and walking away with private opinions there is active debate. Hopefully all will eventually sing in harmony with the designers all the praises associated with the window and its many topics.

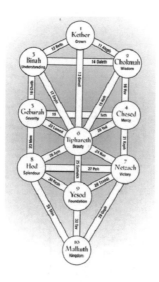

The fenestration of the window is based on the caballa. Netzach is Green. The Minotaur reaches into a seed pod (Capsella bursa pastoris) and this is Yesod. The foundation of new ideas to be sown by the Minotaur.

Bonfire of the Vanities

Bernardino of Siena, OFM (sometimes **Bernardine**) (8th September 1380 – 20th May 1444) was an Italian priest, Franciscan missionary, and is a Catholic Saint. He is known in the Roman Catholic Church as 'the Apostle of Italy' for his efforts to revive the country's Catholic faith during the fifteenth century. His preaching was frequently directed against gambling, witchcraft, sodomy and usury – particularly as practised by Jews.

The focus of this destruction was nominally on objects that might tempt one to sin including vanity items such as mirrors (energies of reflection), cosmetics, fine dresses, playing cards and even musical instruments. Other targets included books that were deemed to be immoral, such as works by Boccacio and manuscripts of secular songs, as well as artworks, including paintings and sculpture.

A key way he destroyed things was on bonfires, so the term Bonfire of the Vanities arose.

Had he known what Botticelli's painting of The Three Graces was really all about, it would have been burnt and the use of the concept of reflection allowed clever designers to put messages on full view but only understood by those who explore the reflections.

Tryst Planting

I am always on the lookout in old landscapes for Tryst Trees. The two Willows at Giverny represented Claude and Camille his lost love. He has hidden her flesh in the willows in some of his works.

He was devastated when they blew over once. The gardeners cut them back and the weight of the roots caused them to re-erect.
MAKE PICTURE BIGGER

Very well I will tell you Madame de Fels, said the devastated Monet.

There was a storm yesterday.It killed two trees in my garden
Two trees , do you hear ? It is not my garden now.It isn't my garden now.
It isn't my gardennow; it's not my garden.

The best example I know of in the UK is in South Park at Darlington.

Hawthorns were commonly used so country lovers could entwine through time.

Grander examples:
A welcome to Bletchley Park

At Parham House, lots of symbolism embraces the landscape.
Another tryst?

Whitchurch Town Twinning. Two oaks are planted in this public open space in Whitchurch and a notice describes how the gap faces Neuvic in the South of France.

Three loved ones are celebrated in this Tryst Seat I designed for our Millennium Green, practical and symbolising three women who, although independent and swimming in their own directions some of the time, combined to provide good support to the community.

The three Alders are Golden.

To the right of where one of Anthony Gormley's men looks, we see two very large trees which 'may' have been a Tryst Planting.

Two brothers in Whitchurch Hampshire were impressed by the triple tryst planting, so they asked for two Alders to go in the churchyard at All Hallows Church, one for late Father and one for late Mother's ashes.

On the site of the ancient Fair in Whitchurch, Hampshire, Fairclose, we have two Yew Trees that may have been a Tryst Planting.

In the centre of Salisbury Cathedral

PROPITIOUS DATES WAS AN ANCIENT CONCEPT
EXAMPLES ARE GIVEN BELOW.

Three Examples of Tuning into
Alignment of Inner Planets

Decimus Burton did design for Palm House at Kew, age forty-four.

'18' is number of Isis. First oxygen O18 not O2. Father was Egyptologist. He gave Decimus first job in 1818 when he was eighteen.

The Holme Regents Park.

44 DEGREE LINK to Temperate House for special reason.

Kathryn of Arragon was an astronomer, astrologer, spoke five languages and gave major donations to women's learning institutions. **Alignment of inner planets when she chose to die due to severe cancer** The only visitors at end of her life were women friends.

IN THE DEEDS OF FULLING MILL, WHITCHURCH, HAMPSHIRE FLOODING INSTRUCTIONS ARE THE WATER MEADOWS TO BEST SERVE SHEEP.

6th September to 14th October inclusive. Thirty-nine days SERVING WATER MEADOW ENRICHMENT.

17th to 25th December inclusive. Eight days Saturnalia Lambing Season SYMBOLIC

5th April to 5th May inclusive. Thirty days SERVING WATER MEADOW ENRICHMENT

Last three days and nights in May. 'Three days' refers to planetary Astrology SYMBOLIC

First four days and nights in June. 'Four days' refers to planetary astrology

William Chambers Applied Special Numerological Thought to the Orangery at Kew

The orangery AT KEW GARDENS now provides public refreshment but it was built to grow plants. The inherent design is interesting. Male and female is needed to grow most creatures and many plants, so the design is built around this in a numerical way.

The white slabs forming the floor are not square. One side is twenty-four inches female and the other is twenty-five inches male.

Count the number of slabs across the orangery and the number along the length.

It is twelve one-way and sixty-eight the other.

Start with the first even number 2 add 2 to make 4 add 4 to the previous number (2) to make 6; add the previous two numbers 2+4+6 = 12. That's the number of slabs in the width.

Now go to the long side and start again with the first odd number 1.

Double it to make 2, two times 2 is 4; 4+2 is 6; 6+4 is 10 (here we go on Fibonacci, a numbering system at the centre of all plant growth); 10 plus 6 is 16; 16 plus 10 is 26; 26 plus 16 is 42; 42plus 26 is 68 and the number of slabs along the long side.

It is twenty-five feet male by one hundred and thirty-six feet female.

DECIMUS BURTON THOUGHT NUMBERS ALSO.

You may have noticed the eighteen diamonds in the Victoria Gate near the shop possibly celebrating the young and beautiful twenty-four-year-old Queen of that name who donated extra land to Kew Gardens.

She died aged eighty-one, as did Decimus.

He died in the year 1881.

Hadspen Intro

It is not until one analyse the words Hadspen Parabola used to describe and English Garden in Somerset, England, that we discover it is not based on the geometry called a Parabola but a Catenary. The layout and numerology associated with geometry and even the brick laying is fascinating.

The astronomical alignments were revealed to me by Charles Barclay of Marlborough College.

This is the walled garden.

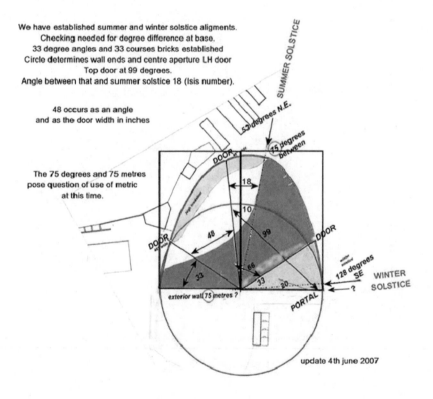

We have established summer and winter solstice aligments.
Checking needed for degree difference at base.
33 degree angles and 33 courses bricks established
Circle determines wall ends and centre aperture LH door
Top door at 99 degrees.
Angle between that and summer solstice 18 (Isis number).

48 occurs as an angle
and as the door width in inches

The 75 degrees and 75 metres
pose question of use of metric
at this time.

update 4th june 2007

HADe susPENded.

The sun's energies and numbers always **contribute to the substance of humanity.**
The Sun's cyclic number and pulse period is ever 11.1 years.

At Hadspen a gyrdan, girdle or fence, makes a garden.
HADE (old word for the angle between a geological bed and the vertical) **SPEN** alludes
Central axis 33 degrees East from North hallow the sun AND TRINITY.
The **catenary**, not parabola, celebrates the emergence of new knowledge,
Angle of the Dangle.
Explained in
1691.
Bernouli-Huygens-Leipniz.
Sun number determines the courses in the sun-receiving walls **(33)**
32 brick, one capping stone.
We may share another reality with the original designers, **33** vertebrae.

Horus and fifteen other leaders reigned **thirty-three** years.
Falcons flew between the sun and the prey, so the sun blinded them for an ancient aerial agriculture. They succeeded as part of a natural cycle, so must we.

His eye was a **measure of grown crops also; every part represented a sense.**

If you dig in deeper by rising higher and looking down at the overall site plan, you will see the alignments arise from a cave to the west. This is in a quarry and possibly the source of the stone to build the house.

A hole in the wall of the cave points to a solar alignment

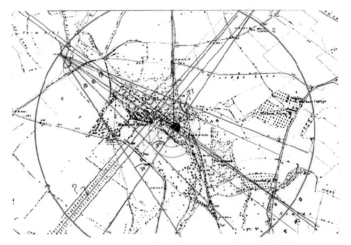

The associated field boundaries may refer to a creature, a pig.

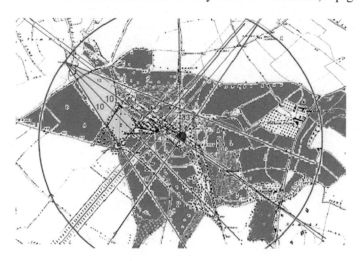

Alluding to Geometry

Remez or hint with regard to Stow and underlying geometry.

57 Consult the genius of the place in all;
58 That tells the waters or to rise, or fall;
59 Or helps th' ambitious hill the heav'ns to scale,
60 Or scoops in circling theatres the vale;
61 Calls in the country, catches opening glades,
62 Joins willing woods, and varies shades from shades,
63 Now breaks, or now directs, th' intending lines;
64 Paints as you plant, and, as you work, designs.
65 Still follow sense, of ev'ry art the soul,
66 Parts answ'ring parts shall slide into a whole,
67 Spontaneous beauties all around advance,
68 Start ev'n from difficulty, strike from chance;
69 Nature shall join you; time shall make it grow
70 A work to wonder at – perhaps a Stowe.

Alexander Pope Stowe
Focus Highlights

1 'Tis strange, the miser should his cares employ
2 To gain those riches he can ne'er enjoy:
3 Is it less strange, the prodigal should waste?
4 His wealth to purchase what he ne'er can taste?
5 Not for himself he sees, or hears, or eats;
6 Artists must choose his pictures, music, meats:
7 He buys for Topham, drawings and designs,
8 For Pembroke, statues, dirty gods, and coins;
9 Rare monkish manuscripts for Hearne alone,
10 And books for Mead, and butterflies for Sloane.
11 Think we all these are for himself? No more
12 Than his fine wife, alas! Or finer whore.
13 For what his Virro painted, built and planted?
14 Only to show, how many tastes he wanted.
15 What brought Sir Visto's ill got wealth to waste?
16 Some daemon whisper'd, "Visto! Have a taste."
17 Heav'n visits with a taste the wealthy fool,
18 And needs no rod but Ripley with a rule.
19 See! Sportive fate, to punish awkward pride,
20 Bids Bubo build, and sends him such a guide:
21 A standing sermon, at each year's expense,
22 That never coxcomb reach'd magnificence!
23 You show us, Rome was glorious, not profuse,
24 And pompous buildings once were things of use.
25 Yet shall (my Lord) your just, your noble rules
26 Fill half the land with imitating fools;
27 Who random drawings from your sheets shall take,
28 And of one beauty many blunders make;
29 Load some vain church with old theatrical state,
30 Turn arcs of triumph to a garden gate;
31 Reverse your ornaments, and hang them all
32 On some patch'd dog-hole ek'd with ends of wall;
33 Then clap four slices of pilaster on't,
34 That lac'd with bits of rustic, makes a front.
35 Or call the winds through long arcades to roar,

36 <u>Proud to catch cold at a Venetian door;</u>
37 <u>Conscious they act a true Palladian part,</u>
38 And, if they starve, they starve by rules of art.
39<u> Oft have you hinted to your brother peer,</u>
40 A certain truth, which many buy too dear:
41 Something there is more needful than expense,
42 And something previous ev'n to taste – 'tis sense:
43 Good sense, which only is the gift of Heav'n,
44 <u>And though no science, fairly worth the sev'n:</u>
45 A light, which in yourself you must perceive;
46 <u>Jones and Le Notre have it not to give.</u>

47<u> To build, to plant, whatever you intend,</u>
48 To rear the column, or the arch to bend,
49 To swell the terrace, or to sink the grot;
50 In all, let Nature never be forgot.
51 But treat the goddess like a modest fair,
52 Nor overdress, nor leave her wholly bare;
53 Let not each beauty ev'rywhere be spied,
54 Where half the skill is decently to hide.
55 <u>He gains all points, who pleasingly confounds,</u>
56 Surprises, varies, and conceals the bounds.
57 Consult the genius of the place in all;
58 That tells the waters or to rise, or fall;
59 Or helps th' ambitious hill the heav'ns to scale,
60 Or scoops in circling theatres the vale;
61 Calls in the country, catches opening glades,
62 Joins willing woods, and varies shades from shades,
63 Now breaks, or now directs, th' intending lines;
64 Paints as you plant, and, as you work, designs.
65 Still follow sense, of ev'ry art the soul,
66 Parts answ'ring parts shall slide into a whole,
67 Spontaneous beauties all around advance,
68 Start ev'n from difficulty, strike from chance;
69 Nature shall join you; time shall make it grow
70 <u>A work to wonder at – perhaps a Stowe.</u>
71<u> Without it, proud Versailles! Thy glory falls;</u>
72 <u>And Nero's terraces desert their walls:</u>
73 The vast parterres a thousand hands shall make,
74 <u>Lo! Cobham comes, and floats them with a lake:</u>
75 <u>Or cut wide views through mountains to the plain,</u>
76 You'll wish your hill or shelter'd seat again.
77 Ev'n in an ornament its place remark,
78 <u>Nor in an hermitage set Dr Clarke.</u>

79 Behold Villario's ten years' toil complete;
80 His quincunx darkens, his espaliers meet;
81 The wood supports the plain, the parts unite,
82 And strength of shade contends with strength of light;
83 A waving glow his bloomy beds display,
84 Blushing in bright diversities of day,
85 With silver-quiv'ring rills meander'd o'er –
86 Enjoy them, you! Villario can no more;
87 Tir'd of the scene parterres and fountains yield,
88 He finds at last he better likes a field.
89 Through his young woods how pleas'd Sabinus stray'd,
90 Or sat delighted in the thick'ning shade,
91 With annual joy the redd'ning shoots to greet,
92 Or see the stretching branches long to meet!
93 His son's fine taste an op'ner vista loves,
94 Foe to the dryads of his father's groves;
95 One boundless green, or flourish'd carpet views,
96 With all the mournful family of yews;
97 The thriving plants ignoble broomsticks made,
98 Now sweep those alleys they were born to shade.
99 At Timon's villa let us pass a day,
100 Where all cry out, "What sums are thrown away!"
101 So proud, so grand of that stupendous air,
102 Soft and agreeable come never there.
103 Greatness, with Timon, dwells in such a draught
104 As brings all Brobdingnag before your thought.
105 To compass this, his building is a town,
106 His pond an ocean, his parterre a down:
107 Who but must laugh, the master when he sees,
108 A puny insect, shiv'ring at a breeze!
109 Lo, what huge heaps of littleness around!
110 The whole, a labour'd quarry above ground.
111 Two cupids squirt before: a lake behind
112 Improves the keenness of the Northern wind.
113 His gardens next your admiration call,
114 On ev'ry side you look, behold the wall!
115 No pleasing intricacies intervene,
116 No artful wildness to perplex the scene;
117 Grove nods at grove, each alley has a brother,
118 And half the platform just reflects the other.
119 The suff'ring eye inverted Nature sees,
120 Trees cut to statues, statues thick as trees;
121 With here a fountain, never to be play'd;
122 And there a summerhouse, that knows no shade;
123 Here Amphitrite sails through myrtle bow'rs;

124 There gladiators fight, or die in flow'rs;
125 Unwater'd see the drooping sea horse mourn,
126 And swallows roost in Nilus' dusty urn.
127 My Lord advances with majestic mien,
128 Smit with the mighty pleasure, to be seen:
129 But soft – by regular approach – not yet –
130 First through the length of yon hot terrace sweat;
131 And when up ten steep slopes you've dragg'd your thighs,
132 Just at his study door he'll bless your eyes.
133 His study! With what authors is it stor'd?
134 In books, not authors, curious is my Lord;
135 To all their dated backs he turns you round:
136 These Aldus printed, those Du Sueil has bound.
137 Lo, some are vellum, and the rest as good
138 For all his Lordship knows, but they are wood.
139 For Locke or Milton 'tis in vain to look,
140 These shelves admit not any modern book.
141 And now the chapel's silver bell you hear,
142 That summons you to all the pride of pray'r:
143 Light quirks of music, broken and uneven,
144 Make the soul dance upon a jig to heaven.
145 On painted ceilings you devoutly stare,
146 Where sprawl the saints of Verrio or Laguerre,
147 On gilded clouds in fair expansion lie,
148 And bring all paradise before your eye.
149 To rest, the cushion and soft dean invite,
150 Who never mentions Hell to ears polite.
151 But hark! The chiming clocks to dinner call;
152 A hundred footsteps scrape the marble hall:
153 The rich buffet well-colour'd serpents grace,
154 And gaping Tritons spew to wash your face.
155 Is this a dinner? This a genial room?
156 No, 'tis a temple, and a hecatomb.
157 A solemn sacrifice, perform'd in state,
158 You drink by measure, and to minutes eat.
159 So quick retires each flying course, you'd swear
160 Sancho's dread doctor and his wand were there.
161 Between each act the trembling salvers ring,
162 From soup to sweet wine, and God bless the King.
163 In plenty starving, tantaliz'd in state,
164 And complaisantly help'd to all I hate,
165 Treated, caress'd, and tir'd, I take my leave,
166 Sick of his civil pride from morn to eve;
167 I curse such lavish cost, and little skill,
168 And swear no day was ever pass'd so ill.

169 <u>Yet hence the poor are cloth'd, the hungry fed;</u>
170 Health to himself, and to his infants bread
171 The lab'rer bears: What his hard heart denies,
172 His charitable vanity supplies.
173 Another age shall see the golden ear
174 Embrown the slope, and nod on the parterre,
175 Deep harvests bury all his pride has plann'd,
176 <u>And laughing Ceres reassume the land.</u>
177 Who then shall grace, or who improve the soil?
178 <u>Who plants like Bathurst, or who builds like Boyle.</u>
179 'Tis use alone that sanctifies expense,
180 And splendour borrows all her rays from sense.
181 His father's acres who enjoys in peace,
182 Or makes his neighbours glad, if he increase:
183 Whose cheerful tenants bless their yearly toil,
184 Yet to their Lord owe more than to the soil;
185 Whose ample lawns are not asham'd to feed
186 The milky heifer and deserving steed;
187 Whose rising forests, not for pride or show,
188 But future buildings, future navies, grow:
189 Let his plantations stretch from down to down,
190 First shade a country, and then raise a town.
191 You too proceed! Make falling arts your care,
192 Erect new wonders, and the old repair;
193 Jones and Palladio to themselves restore,
194 <u>And be whate'er Vitruvius was before:</u>
195 <u>Till kings call forth th' ideas of your mind,</u>
196 Proud to accomplish what such hands design'd,
197 Bid harbours open, public ways extend,
198 Bid temples, worthier of the God, ascend;
199 Bid the broad arch the dang'rous flood contain,
200 The mole projected breaks the roaring main;
201 Back to his bounds their subject sea command,
202 And roll obedient rivers through the land;
203 These honours, peace to happy Britain brings,
204 These are imperial works, and worthy kings.
Notes:
<u>1]</u> Published in December 1731

Alexander Pope Stowe Plus

1 'Tis strange, the miser should his cares employ
2 To gain those riches he can ne'er enjoy:
3 Is it less strange, the prodigal should waste
4 His wealth to purchase what he ne'er can taste?
5 Not for himself he sees, or hears, or eats;
6 Artists must choose his pictures, music, meats:
7 He buys for Topham, drawings and designs,
8 For Pembroke, statues, dirty gods, and coins;
9 Rare monkish manuscripts for Hearne alone,
10 And books for Mead, and butterflies for Sloane.
11 Think we all these are for himself? No more
12 Than his fine wife, alas! Or finer whore.
13 For what his Virro painted, built and planted?
14 Only to show, how many tastes he wanted.
15 What brought Sir Visto's ill got wealth to waste?
16 Some daemon whisper'd, "Visto! Have a taste."
17 Heav'n visits with a taste the wealthy fool,
18 And needs no rod but Ripley with a rule.
19 See! Sportive fate, to punish awkward pride,
20 Bids Bubo build, and sends him such a guide:
21 A standing sermon, at each year's expense,
22 That never coxcomb reach'd magnificence!
23 You show us, Rome was glorious, not profuse,
24 And pompous buildings once were things of use.
25 Yet shall (my Lord) your just, your noble rules
26 Fill half the land with imitating fools;
27 Who random drawings from your sheets shall take,
28 And of one beauty many blunders make;
29 Load some vain church with old theatric state,
30 Turn arcs of triumph to a garden gate;
31 Reverse your ornaments, and hang them all
32 On some patch'd dog-hole ek'd with ends of wall;
33 Then clap four slices of pilaster on't,
34 That lac'd with bits of rustic, makes a front.
35 Or call the winds through long arcades to roar,
36 Proud to catch cold at a Venetian door;
37 Conscious they act a true Palladian part,

38 And, if they starve, they starve by rules of art.
39 Oft have you hinted to your brother peer,
40 A certain truth, which many buy too dear:
41 Something there is more needful than expense,
42 And something previous ev'n to taste – 'tis sense:
43 Good sense, which only is the gift of Heav'n,
44 And though no science, fairly worth the sev'n:
45 A light, which in yourself you must perceive;
46 Jones and Le Notre have it not to give.
47 To build, to plant, whatever you intend,
48 To rear the column, or the arch to bend,
49 To swell the terrace, or to sink the grot;
50 In all, let Nature never be forgot.
51 But treat the goddess like a modest fair,
52 Nor overdress, nor leave her wholly bare;
53 Let not each beauty ev'rywhere be spied,
54 Where half the skill is decently to hide.
55 He gains all points, who pleasingly confounds,
56 Surprises, varies, and conceals the bounds.
57 Consult the genius of the place in all;
58 That tells the waters or to rise, or fall;
59 Or helps th' ambitious hill the heav'ns to scale,
60 Or scoops in circling theatres the vale;
61 Calls in the country, catches opening glades,
62 Joins willing woods, and varies shades from shades,
63 Now breaks, or now directs, th' intending lines;
64 Paints as you plant, and, as you work, designs.
65 Still follow sense, of ev'ry art the soul,
66 Parts answ'ring parts shall slide into a whole,
67 Spontaneous beauties all around advance,
68 Start ev'n from difficulty, strike from chance;
69 Nature shall join you; time shall make it grow
70 A work to wonder at – perhaps a Stowe.
71 Without it, proud Versailles! Thy glory falls;
72 And Nero's terraces desert their walls:
73 The vast parterres a thousand hands shall make,
74 Lo! Cobham comes, and floats them with a lake:
75 Or cut wide views through mountains to the plain,
76 You'll wish your hill or shelter'd seat again.
77 Ev'n in an ornament its place remark,
78 Nor in an hermitage set Dr Clarke.
79 Behold Villario's ten years' toil complete;
80 His quincunx darkens, his espaliers meet;
81 The wood supports the plain, the parts unite,
82 And strength of shade contends with strength of light;

83 A waving glow his bloomy beds display,
84 Blushing in bright diversities of day,
85 With silver-quiv'ring rills meander'd o'er –
86 Enjoy them, you! Villario can no more;
87 Tir'd of the scene parterres and fountains yield,
88 He finds at last he better likes a field.
89 Through his young woods how pleas'd Sabinus stray'd,
90 Or sat delighted in the thick'ning shade,
91 With annual joy the redd'ning shoots to greet,
92 Or see the stretching branches long to meet!
93 His son's fine taste an op'ner vista loves,
94 Foe to the dryads of his father's groves;
95 One boundless green, or flourish'd carpet views,
96 With all the mournful family of yews;
97 The thriving plants ignoble broomsticks made,
98 Now sweep those alleys they were born to shade.
99 At Timon's villa let us pass a day,
100 Where all cry out, "What sums are thrown away!"
101 So proud, so grand of that stupendous air,
102 Soft and agreeable come never there.
103 Greatness, with Timon, dwells in such a draught
104 As brings all Brobdingnag before your thought.
105 To compass this, his building is a town,
106 His pond an ocean, his parterre a down:
107 Who but must laugh, the master when he sees,
108 A puny insect, shiv'ring at a breeze!
109 Lo, what huge heaps of littleness around!
110 The whole, a labour'd quarry above ground.
111 Two cupids squirt before: a lake behind
112 Improves the keenness of the Northern wind.
113 His gardens next your admiration call,
114 On ev'ry side you look, behold the wall!
115 No pleasing intricacies intervene,
116 No artful wildness to perplex the scene;
117 Grove nods at grove, each alley has a brother,
118 And half the platform just reflects the other.
119 The suff'ring eye inverted Nature sees,
120 Trees cut to statues, statues thick as trees;
121 With here a fountain, never to be play'd;
122 And there a summerhouse, that knows no shade;
123 Here Amphitrite sails through myrtle bow'rs;
124 There gladiators fight, or die in flow'rs;
125 Unwater'd see the drooping sea horse mourn,
126 And swallows roost in Nilus' dusty urn.
127 My Lord advances with majestic mien,

128 Smit with the mighty pleasure, to be seen:
129 But soft – by regular approach – not yet –
130 First through the length of yon hot terrace sweat;
131 And when up ten steep slopes you've dragg'd your thighs,
132 Just at his study door he'll bless your eyes.
133 His study! With what authors is it stor'd?
134 In books, not authors, curious is my Lord;
135 To all their dated backs he turns you round:
136 These Aldus printed, those Du Sueil has bound.
137 Lo, some are vellum, and the rest as good
138 For all his Lordship knows, but they are wood.
139 For Locke or Milton 'tis in vain to look,
140 These shelves admit not any modern book.
141 And now the chapel's silver bell you hear,
142 That summons you to all the pride of pray'r:
143 Light quirks of music, broken and uneven,
144 Make the soul dance upon a jig to heaven.
145 On painted ceilings you devoutly stare,
146 Where sprawl the saints of Verrio or Laguerre,
147 On gilded clouds in fair expansion lie,
148 And bring all paradise before your eye.
149 To rest, the cushion and soft dean invite,
150 Who never mentions Hell to ears polite.
151 But hark! The chiming clocks to dinner call;
152 A hundred footsteps scrape the marble hall:
153 The rich buffet well-colour'd serpents grace,
154 And gaping Tritons spew to wash your face.
155 Is this a dinner? This a genial room?
156 No, 'tis a temple, and a hecatomb.
157 A solemn sacrifice, perform'd in state,
158 You drink by measure, and to minutes eat.
159 So quick retires each flying course, you'd swear
160 Sancho's dread doctor and his wand were there.
161 Between each act the trembling salvers ring,
162 From soup to sweet wine, and God bless the King.
163 In plenty starving, tantaliz'd in state,
164 And complaisantly help'd to all I hate,
165 Treated, caress'd, and tir'd, I take my leave,
166 Sick of his civil pride from morn to eve;
167 I curse such lavish cost, and little skill,
168 And swear no day was ever pass'd so ill.
169 Yet hence the poor are cloth'd, the hungry fed;
170 Health to himself, and to his infants bread
171 The lab'rer bears: What his hard heart denies,
172 His charitable vanity supplies.

173 Another age shall see the golden ear
174 Embrown the slope, and nod on the parterre,
175 Deep harvests bury all his pride has plann'd,
176 <u>And laughing Ceres reassume the land.</u>
177 Who then shall grace, or who improve the soil?
178 <u>Who plants like Bathurst, or who builds like Boyle.</u>
179 'Tis use alone that sanctifies expense,
180 And splendour borrows all her rays from sense.
181 His father's acres who enjoys in peace,
182 Or makes his neighbours glad, if he increase:
183 Whose cheerful tenants bless their yearly toil,
184 Yet to their Lord owe more than to the soil;
185 Whose ample lawns are not asham'd to feed
186 The milky heifer and deserving steed;
187 Whose rising forests, not for pride or show,
188 But future buildings, future navies, grow:
189 Let his plantations stretch from down to down,
190 First shade a country, and then raise a town.
191 You too proceed! Make falling arts your care,
192 Erect new wonders, and the old repair;
193 Jones and Palladio to themselves restore,
194 <u>And be whate'er Vitruvius was before:</u>
195 <u>Till kings call forth th' ideas of your mind,</u>
196 Proud to accomplish what such hands design'd,
197 Bid harbours open, public ways extend,
198 Bid temples, worthier of the God, ascend;
199 Bid the broad arch the dang'rous flood contain,
200 The mole projected breaks the roaring main;
201 Back to his bounds their subject sea command,
202 And roll obedient rivers through the land;
203 These honours, peace to happy Britain brings,
204 These are imperial works, and worthy kings.

Notes
Published in December 1731

Henry Wotton's Poem

How happy is he born and taught
That serveth not another's will;
Whose armour is his honest thought,
And simple truth his utmost skill!
Whose passions not his masters are;
Whose soul is still prepared for death,
Untied unto the world by care
Of public fame or private breath;
Who envies none that chance doth raise,
Nor vice; who never understood
How deepest wounds are given by praise;
Nor rules of state, but rules of good;
Who hath his life from rumours freed;
Whose conscience is his strong retreat;
Whose state can neither flatterers feed,
Nor ruin make oppressors great;
Who God doth late and early pray
More of His grace than gifts to lend;
And entertains the harmless day
With a religious book or friend;
This man is freed from servile bands
Of hope to rise or fear to fall:
Lord of himself, though not of lands,
And having nothing, yet hath all.

Waterford Intro

Your celebration of ISIS and total creativity was very simply achieved through numerology Decimus, but I am wondering if you and your colleagues discussed other manifestations like what I discovered on a visit to Waterford Bay?

Her husband was kidnapped and chopped into fifteen pieces, another symbolic number, odd like all male numbers and that of the Green man. So total fertility. After a long search, she found him and re-assembled her loved one. The final part of his body was his penis and once that was in place, life could go on.

Was the layout of the landscape at Waterford a coincidence or did those in control of the landscape tune into special dynamics. Key ones the flows of rivers and streams and the shaping of field systems?

Water Gate

ISIS

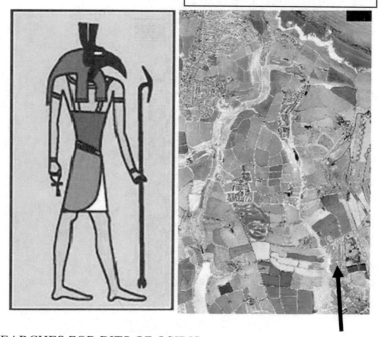

ISIS SEARCHES FOR BITS OF OSIRIS.

MILITARY CAMP VERY MALE

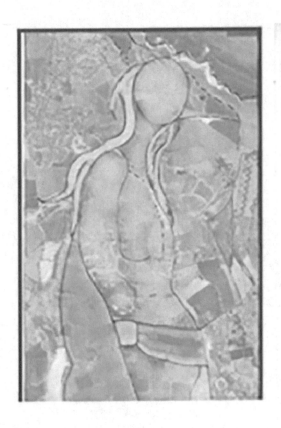

HAVING ACHIEVED LUNAR COMPLETION, SHE
HAS fourteen PIECES.

SHE FINALLY CONNECTS WITH THE fifteenth PIECE AND LIFE GOES
ON.

Abridged CV

Graham Burgess has a long experience and impeccable success record of creating landscapes on many levels with key skills at tuning into the needs of discerning clients.

Student at The Royal Botanic Gardens Kew

Onetime Supervisor of Arboretum South at The Royal Botanic Gardens Kew. This led to foundations for application of plant skills worldwide. Member of Education and Publicity Committee of The Arboricultural Association (National body re tree care)

He led an expedition to the jungles of South America.

Director with The John Lewis Partnership. Responsibilities included landscaping round shops, factories, warehouses covering functional car parks for Waitrose shoppers and staff. It included roof-gardens. Responsibilities included some of finest gardens in UK, Brownsea Castle, Odney Club Cookham, Leckford Abbas and Longstock Park, the finest water-garden in the world. Work associated with golf courses. Also, he ran hardy nursery stock nursery and ended up Chairman of The Horticultural Trades Association for Hampshire, Dorset and Isle of Wight (biggest branch in UK).

He formed Artscapes a design and built business and Artscapes Aqua a specialist nursery growing aquatic plants.

Tropical expertise applied designing landscape for Schroder Wag in Tortola, British Virgin Islands and landscape around Commercial Centre, Puerto del Carmen, Lanzarote.

TSB headquarters Andover Hampshire included car parks, high-quality landscape and optimal relationship to river running through site.

Won Premiere Prize at our only International Garden Festival in Liverpool with The Beatles Maze. Major sponsors sourced. Landscaped all lakes and played key roles in Canadian Garden and Kew Garden.

Subsequently, he landscaped all lakes at all Garden Festivals countrywide.

He landscaped lakes at Stockley Business Park; Chiswick Business Park and many others.

He won acclaim at Chelsea Flower Show, last show there for The Sunday Times. Another garden sponsored by a major investment company had a large lump of Clogau Gold in the centre of a maze.

He entered into area of brand name reinforcement in most competitive area of market namely national shows. He worked with Christian Aid and first feature at Hampton Court Palace Flower Show seen by one billion people worldwide.

Greatest success for them one year at *BBC Gardeners World Live* at National Exhibition Centre in Birmingham gained 65% of all media value at the show

Educational Skills applied to serve Millennium Green Trust, Whitchurch 7.5 acres water meadows (won green flag award) and schools (Geological garden)

He is a specialist in historic gardens. Master Plans for Littlecote Manor (Peter de Savary); Laverstoke Park (Jody Scheckter). He did Lord Bath's favourite labyrinth, The Labyrinth of Love at Longleat. Beazer Maze has pathway of Bath stone and central mosaic made from tesserae from same quarries as used by Michaelangelo for The Sistine Chapel. He invented new technique for pre-fabricating mosaics. Kentwell Hall maze won Heritage Award. Onetime Trustee of The Living Rain Forest, Newbury and The Whitchurch Silk Mill. Currently Director Whitchurch Arts.

Big lakes, e.g. one for Sheikh Maktoum at Windlesham Moor and one for Lord and Lady Remnant.

Exported rarest plants in UK monthly to shop in Paris and also supplied the water lilies for Claude Monet's garden at Giverny. He involved with reed-beds at Magna Park, Lutterworth, one of biggest warehouse distribution centres in UK. Effluent purification. Built own Grand Designs Sustainable House 1997. Collaborative design in California

Some experience in movie making. Recent one celebrating Her Majesty's visits to Whitchurch in 1949 with the Duke before she was crowned. Her Majesty was very pleased with the movie also with the Kathryn of Arragon garden which was done at invitation of The Royal Horticultural Society as part of six wives of Henry the Eighth. It was designed for any Queen. He got more seconds on TV than any other garden at the show at Hampton Court. He presented to HMQ 2015 at Buckingham Palace as Chair for the South of Winston Churchill Travel Fellowship.

Key is integrating the psychologies that affect all user relationships with landscape and bringing together expertise on many levels to produce a pleasing and cost-effective end result.

So he had a lifetime involved in close contact with nature in plants and the forces that encourage them to grow. Experience in locations filled with historic symbolism on many levels including numerology and special geometries. Skilled in industrial psychology and advertising and this depends on linking effectively on sub-conscious and conscious levels with human beings of all ages, races and cultures.

I WANT TO FINISH THIS BOOK WITH A MESSAGE:

The letter S means 'being of the flesh' as explained in the chapter on letters. So KISS, CARESS?

If you bring two together in a balanced and palindromic way, this is what appears.

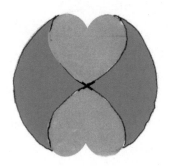

Two hearts, and where they meet in the centre the kiss we put at the end of special messages.

The hidden geometry hints at the *labrys*, the double-headed axe of the Minoans and a symbol of quick change.

Want to live with it? Buy a Claddagh Ring.